MABINOGION
TALES

MABINOGION
TALES

translated by

CHARLOTTE GUEST

edited by

OWEN EDWARDS

illustrations prepared by

JO NATHAN

published in 1991
by Llanerch, Felinfach.

ISBN 0947992 73 1

Introduction.

Lady Charlotte Guest has given *The Mabinogion* to English readers in the form which, probably, will ever most delight them. Her transcript of the Red Book of Hergest was not perfect, she found the meaning of many a Welsh phrase obscure, but her rendering is generally very accurate; and the Celtic tales retain in their new dress much of the charm, which so often evades a translator, of a perfect style formed by generations of narrating.

The Red Book of Hergest, from which *The Mabinogion* are taken, is a collection of tales and poems written during the fourteenth century. Some of the Mabinogion in it have been reconstructed in Norman and Crusading times, but they contain reminiscences of a more distant period, often but half understood by the later story-teller. Among these are The Dream of Rhonabwy, and The Lady of the Fountain. These are Christian, but with distant glimpses of Celtic heathenism. The adventures are grouped around Arthur and his knights; and a kind of connection is given to the tales by the presence of Owen and his mysterious ravens. Some other Mabinogion tales are far older; older than Christianity and Arthur.

In this edition of Lady Guest's translation I have put, in the form of footnotes, what appears to me to be a more correct or literal rendering of some of the passages of the Welsh. This course makes it unnecessary to tamper with the charming translation that has become a classic of the English language.

OWEN EDWARDS

Lincoln College, Oxford, 1st. March 1902.

Contents

GERAINT THE SON OF ERBIN.

ARTHUR was accustomed to hold his Court at Caerlleon upon Usk. And there he held it seven Easters,[1] and five Christmases. And once upon a time he held his Court there at Whitsuntide. For Caerlleon was the place most easy of access in his dominions, both by sea and by land. And there were assembled[2] nine crowned kings, who were his

---

[1] Add "successively." [2] And he summoned to him.

tributaries, and likewise earls and barons. For they were his invited guests at all the high festivals, unless they were prevented by any great hindrance. And when he was at Caerlleon, holding his Court, thirteen churches were set apart for mass. And thus were they appointed: one church for Arthur, and his kings, and his guests; and the second for Gwenhwyvar and her ladies; and the third for the Steward of the Household and the Suitors; and the fourth for the Franks, and the other officers; and the other nine churches were for the nine Masters of the Household, and chiefly for Gwalchmai; for he, from the eminence of his warlike fame, and from the nobleness of his birth, was the most exalted of the nine. And there was no other arrangement respecting the churches than that which we have mentioned above.

Glewlwyd Gavaelvawr was the chief porter; but he did not himself perform the office, except at one of the three high festivals, for he had seven men to serve him; and they divided the year amongst them. They were Grynn, and Pen Pighon, and Llaes Cymyn, and Gogyfwlch, and Gwrdnei with Cat's eyes, who could see as well by night as by day, and Drem the son of Dremhitid, and Clust the son of Clustveinyd; and these were Arthur's guards. And on Whit Tuesday, as the King sat at the banquet, lo! there entered a tall, fair-headed youth, clad in a coat and a surcoat of diapred satin, and a golden-hilted sword about his neck, and low shoes of leather upon his feet. And he came, and stood before Arthur. "Hail to thee, Lord!" said he. "Heaven prosper thee," he answered, "and be thou welcome. Dost thou bring any new tidings?" "I do, Lord," he said. "I know thee not," said Arthur. "It is a

marvel to me that thou dost not know me. I am
one of thy foresters, Lord, in the Forest of Dean, and
my name is Madawc, the son of Twrgadarn." "Tell
me thine errand," said Arthur. "I will do so, Lord,"
said he. "In the Forest I saw a stag, the like of
which beheld I never yet." "What is there about
him," asked Arthur, "that thou never yet didst see
his like?" "He is of pure white, Lord, and he does
not herd with any other animal through stateliness
and pride, so royal is his bearing. And I come to
seek thy counsel, Lord, and to know thy will concerning him." "It seems best to me," said Arthur, "to
go and hunt him to-morrow at break of day; and to
cause general notice thereof to be given to-night in
all quarters of the Court." And Arryfuerys was
Arthur's chief huntsman, and Arelivri was his chief
page. And all received notice; and thus it was
arranged. And they sent the youth before them.
Then Gwenhwyvar said to Arthur, "Wilt thou permit me, Lord," said she, " to go to-morrow to see and
hear the hunt of the stag of which the young man
spoke?" "I will, gladly," said Arthur. "Then will
I go," said she. And Gwalchmai said to Arthur,
" Lord, if it seem well to thee, permit that into whose
hunt soever the stag shall come, that one, be he
a knight or one on foot, may cut off his head, and
give it to whom he pleases, whether to his own lady-
love, or to the lady of his friend." "I grant it
gladly," said Arthur, "and let the Steward of the
Household be chastised if all are not ready to-morrow
for the chase."

And they passed the night with songs, and diversions, and discourse, and ample entertainment. And
when it was time for them all to go to sleep, they
went. And when the next day came, they arose;

and Arthur called the attendants, who guarded his couch. And these were four pages, whose names were Cadyrnerth the son of Porthawr Gandwy, and Ambreu the son of Bedwor, and Amhar, the son of Arthur, and Goreu the son of Custennin. And these men came to Arthur, and saluted him, and arrayed him in his garments. And Arthur wondered that Gwenhwyvar did not awake, and did not move in her bed : and the attendants wished to awaken her. "Disturb her not," said Arthur, "for she had rather sleep than go to see the hunting."

Then Arthur went forth, and he heard two horns sounding, one from near the lodging of the chief huntsman, and the other from near that of the chief page. And the whole assembly of the multitudes came to Arthur, and they took the road to the Forest.

And after Arthur had gone forth from the palace, Gwenhwyvar awoke, and called to her maidens, and apparelled herself. "Maidens," said she, "I had leave last night to go and see the hunt. Go one of you to the stable, and order hither a horse such as a woman may ride." And one of them went, and she found but two horses in the stable, and Gwenhwyvar and one of her maidens mounted them, and went through the Usk, and followed the track of the men and the horses. And as they rode thus, they heard a loud and rushing sound; and they looked behind them, and beheld a knight upon a [1] hunter foal of mighty size ; and the rider was a fair-haired youth, bare-legged, and of princely mien, and a golden-hilted sword was at his side, and a robe and a surcoat of satin were upon him, and two low shoes of leather upon his feet; and around him was a scarf of blue

[1] Add "bespattered."

purple, at each corner of which was a golden apple. And his horse stepped stately, and swift, and proud; and he overtook Gwenhwyvar, and saluted her. "Heaven prosper thee, Geraint," said she, "I knew thee when first I saw thee just now. And the welcome of heaven be unto thee. And why didst thou not go with thy Lord to hunt?" "Because I knew not when he went," said he. "I marvel too," said she, "how he could go unknown to me." "Indeed, lady," said he. "I was fast asleep, and knew not when he went; but thou, O young man, art the most agreeable companion I could have in the whole kingdom; and it may be that I shall be more amused with the hunting than they;[1] for we shall hear the horns when they sound, and we shall hear the dogs when they are let loose, and begin to cry." So they went to the edge of the Forest, and there they stood. "From this place," said she, "we shall hear when the dogs are let loose." And thereupon they heard a loud noise, and they looked towards the spot whence it came, and they beheld a dwarf riding upon a horse, stately, and foaming, and prancing, and strong, and spirited. And in the hand of the dwarf was a whip. And near the dwarf they saw a lady upon a beautiful white horse, of steady and stately pace; and she was clothed in a garment of gold brocade. And near her was a knight upon a war-horse of large size, with heavy and bright armour both upon himself and upon his horse. And truly they never before saw a knight, or a horse, or armour, of such remarkable size. And they were all near to each other.

"Geraint," said Gwenhwyvar, "knowest thou the

---

[1] And it may be that I shall have as much entertainment on account of the hunting as they.

name of that tall knight yonder?" "I know him
not," said he, "and the strange armour that he
wears prevents my either seeing his face or his
features." "Go, maiden," said Gwenhwyvar, "and
ask the dwarf who that knight is." Then the maiden
went up to the dwarf; and the dwarf waited for the
maiden, when he saw her coming towards him. And
the maiden enquired of the dwarf who the knight
was. "I will not tell thee," he answered. "Since
thou art so churlish as not to tell me," said she, "I
will ask him himself." "Thou shalt not ask him, by
my faith," said he. "Wherefore?" said she. "Because thou art not of honour sufficient to befit thee
to speak to my Lord." Then the maiden turned her
horse's head towards the knight, upon which the
dwarf struck her with the whip that was in his hand
across the face and the eyes, until the blood flowed
forth. And the maiden, through the hurt she received from the blow, returned to Gwenhwyvar, complaining of the pain. "Very rudely has the dwarf
treated thee," said Geraint. "I will go myself to
know who the knight is." "Go," said Gwenhwyvar.
And Geraint went up to the dwarf. "Who is yonder
knight?" said Geraint. "I will not tell thee," said
the dwarf. "Then will I ask him himself," said he.
"That wilt thou not, by my faith," said the dwarf;
"thou art not honourable enough to speak with my
Lord." Said Geraint, "I have spoken with men of
equal rank with him." And he turned his horse's
head towards the knight, but the dwarf overtook him
and struck him as he had done the maiden, so that
the blood coloured the scarf that Geraint wore. Then
Geraint put his hand upon the hilt of his sword, but
he took counsel with himself, and considered that it
would be no vengeance for him to slay the dwarf,

and to be attacked unarmed by the armed knight, so he returned to where Gwenhwyvar was.

"Thou hast acted wisely and discreetly," said she. "Lady," said he, "I will follow him yet, with thy permission; and at last he will come to some in-habited place, where I may have arms either as a loan or for a pledge, so that I may encounter the knight." "Go," said she, "and do not attack him until thou hast good arms, and I shall be very anxious concerning thee, until I hear tidings of thee." "If I am alive," said he, "thou shalt hear tidings of me by to-morrow afternoon;" and with that he departed.

And the road they took was below the palace of Caerlleon, and across the ford of the Usk; and they went along a fair, and even, and lofty ridge of ground, until they came to a town, and at the extremity of the town they saw a Fortress and a Castle. And they came to the extremity of the town. And as the knight passed through it, all the people arose, and saluted him, and bade him welcome. And when Geraint came into the town, he looked at every house, to see if he knew any of those whom he saw. But he knew none, and none knew him to do him the kindness to let him have arms either as a loan or for a pledge. And every house he saw was full of men, and arms, and horses. And they were polishing shields, and burnishing swords, and washing armour, and shoeing horses. And the knight, and the lady, and the dwarf, rode up to the Castle that was in the town, and every one was glad in the Castle. And from the battlements and the gates they risked their necks, through their eagerness to greet them, and to show their joy.

Geraint stood there to see whether the knight

would remain in the Castle ; and when he was certain
that he would do so, he looked around him ; and at
a little distance from the town he saw an old palace
in ruins, wherein was a hall that was falling to decay.
And as he knew not any one in the town, he went
towards the old palace ; and when he came near to
the palace, he saw but one chamber, and a bridge of
marble-stone leading to it. And upon the bridge he
saw sitting a hoary-headed man, upon whom were
tattered garments. And Geraint gazed steadfastly
upon him for a long time. Then the hoary-headed
man spoke to him. "Young man," he said, "wherefore art thou thoughtful?" "I am thoughtful," said
he, "because I know not where to go to-night."
"Wilt thou come forward this way, chieftain?" said
he, "and thou shalt have of the best that can be
procured for thee." So Geraint went forward. And
the hoary-headed man preceded him into the hall.
And in the hall he dismounted, and he left there his
horse. Then he went on to the upper chamber with
the hoary-headed man. And in the chamber he
beheld an old decrepit woman, sitting on a cushion,
with old tattered garments of satin upon her ; and it
seemed to him that he had never seen a woman
fairer than she must have been when in the fulness
of youth. And beside her was a maiden, upon whom
were a vest and a veil, that were old, and beginning
to be worn out. And truly he never saw a maiden
more full of comeliness, and grace, and beauty, than
she. And the hoary-headed man said to the maiden,
"There is no attendant for the horse of this youth
but thyself." "I will render the best service I am
able," said she, "both to him and to his horse."
And the maiden disarrayed the youth, and then she
furnished his horse with straw and with corn. And

she went to the hall as before, and then she returned
to the chamber. And the hoary-headed man said to
the maiden, "Go to the town," said he, "and bring
hither the best that thou canst find both of food and
of liquor." "I will, gladly, Lord," said she. And
to the town went the maiden. And they conversed
together, while the maiden was at the town. And,
behold! the maiden came back, and a youth with
her, bearing on his back a costrel full of good
purchased mead and a quarter of a young bullock.
And in the hands of the maiden was a quantity of
white bread, and she had some manchet bread in
her veil, and she came into the chamber. "I could
not obtain better than this," said she, "nor with
better should I have been trusted."   "It is good
enough," said Geraint. And they caused the meat to
be boiled; and when their food was ready, they sat
down. And it was in this wise ; Geraint sat between
the hoary-headed man and his wife, and the maiden
served them. And they ate and drank.

And when they had finished eating, Geraint talked
with the hoary-headed man, and he asked him in the
first place, to whom belonged the Palace that he was
in. "Truly," said he, "it was I that built it, and to
me also belonged the city and the castle which thou
sawest." "Alas!" said Geraint, "how is it that
thou hast lost them now?" "I lost a great Earldom
as well as these," said he, "and this is how I lost
them. I had a nephew, the son of my brother, and
I took his possessions to myself; and when he came
to his strength, he demanded of me his property, but
I withheld it from him. So he made war upon me,
and wrested from me all that I possessed." "Good,
Sir,[1] said Geraint, "wilt thou tell me wherefore came

---

[1] Good Sir.

the knight, and the lady, and the dwarf, just now into the town, and what is the preparation which I saw, and the putting of arms in order." "I will do so," said he. "The preparations are for the game that is to be held, to-morrow by the young Earl, which will be on this wise. In the midst of a meadow which is here, two forks will be set up, and upon the two forks a silver rod, and upon the silver rod a Sparrow-Hawk, and for the Sparrow-Hawk there will be a tournament. And to the tournament will go all the array thou didst see in the city, of men, and of horses, and of arms. And with each man will go the lady he loves best; and no man can joust for the Sparrow-Hawk, except the lady he loves best be with him. And the knight that thou sawest has gained the Sparrow-Hawk these two years; and if he gains it the third year, they will, from that time, send it every year to him, and he himself will come here no more. And he will be called the knight of the Sparrow-Hawk from that time forth." "Sir," said Geraint, "what is thy counsel to me concerning this knight, on account of the insult which I received from the dwarf, and that which was received by the maiden of Gwenhwyvar, the wife of Arthur?" And Geraint told the hoary-headed man what the insult was that he had received. "It is not easy to counsel thee, inasmuch as thou hast neither dame nor maiden belonging to thee, for whom thou canst joust. Yet, I have arms here, which thou couldest have; and there is my horse also, if he seem to thee better than thine own."

"Ah! Sir," said he, "Heaven reward thee. But my own horse, to which I am accustomed, together with thine arms, will suffice me. And if, when the appointed time shall come to-morrow, thou wilt permit me, Sir, to challenge for yonder maiden that is thy daughter, I will engage, if I escape from the tournament, to love the maiden as long as I live, and if I do not escape, she will remain unsullied as before." "Gladly will I permit thee," said the hoary-headed man, "and since thou dost thus resolve, it is necessary that thy horse and arms should be ready to-morrow at break of day. For then, the knight of the Sparrow-Hawk will make proclamation, and ask the lady he loves best to take the Sparrow-Hawk. 'For,' will he say to her, 'thou art the fairest of women, and thou didst possess it last year, and the year previous; and if any deny it thee to-day, by force will I defend it for thee.' And therefore," said the hoary-headed man, "it is needful for thee to be there at daybreak, and we three will be with thee," and thus was it settled.

And at night, lo![1] they went to sleep; and before the dawn they arose, and arrayed themselves; and by the time that it was day, they were all four in the meadow. And there was the knight of the Sparrow-Hawk making the proclamation, and asking his lady-love to fetch the Sparrow-Hawk. "Fetch it not," said Geraint, "for there is here a maiden, who is fairer, and more noble, and more comely, and who has a better claim to it than thou." "If thou maintainest the Sparrow-Hawk to be due to her, come forward, and do battle with me." And Geraint went forward to the top of the meadow, having upon himself and upon his horse armour which was heavy, and rusty, and worthless, and of uncouth shape. Then they encountered each other, and they broke a set of lances, and they broke a second set, and a third. And thus they did at every onset, and they broke as many lances as were brought to

[1] There.

B

them. And when the Earl and his company saw
the knight of the Sparrow-Hawk gaining the mastery,
there was shouting, and joy, and mirth amongst
them. And the hoary-headed man, and his wife,
and his daughter, were sorrowful. And the hoary-
headed man served Geraint lances as often as he
broke them, and the dwarf served the knight of the

Sparrow-Hawk. Then the hoary-headed man came
to Geraint. "Oh! chieftain," said he, "since no
other will hold with thee, behold, here is the lance
which was in my hand on the day when I received
the honour of knighthood; and from that time to
this I never broke it. And it has an excellent point."
Then Geraint took the lance, thanking the hoary-

headed man. And thereupon the dwarf also brought a lance to his lord. "Behold here is a lance for thee, not less good than his," said the dwarf. "And bethink thee, that no knight ever withstood thee before so long as this one has done." "I declare to Heaven," said Geraint, "that unless death takes me quickly hence, he shall fare never the better for thy service." And Geraint pricked his horse towards him from afar, and warning him, he rushed upon him, and gave him a blow so severe, and furious, and fierce, upon the face of his shield, that he cleft it in two, and broke his armour, and burst his girths, so that both he and his saddle were borne to the ground over the horse's crupper. And Geraint dismounted quickly. And he was wroth, and he drew his sword, and rushed fiercely upon him. Then the knight also arose, and drew his sword against Geraint. And they fought on foot with their swords until their arms struck sparks of fire like stars from one another; and thus they continued fighting until the blood and sweat obscured the light from their eyes. And when Geraint prevailed, the hoary-headed man, and his wife, and his daughter were glad; and when the knight prevailed, it rejoiced the Earl and his party. Then the hoary-headed man saw Geraint receive a severe stroke, and he went up to him quickly, and said to him, "Oh, chieftain, remember the treatment which thou hadst from the dwarf; and wilt thou not seek vengeance for the insult to thyself, and for the insult to Gwenhwyvar the wife of Arthur!" And Geraint was roused by what he said to him,[1] and he called to him all his strength, and lifted up his sword, and struck the knight upon the crown of his head, so that he broke all his head armour, and cut through

---

[1] And his words reached Geraint.

all the flesh and the skin, even to the skull, until he wounded the bone.

Then the knight fell upon his knees, and cast his sword from his hand, and besought mercy of Geraint. "Of a truth," said he, "I relinquish my overdaring and my pride in craving thy mercy; and unless I have time to commit myself to Heaven for my sins, and to talk with a priest, thy mercy will avail me little." "I will grant thee grace upon this condition," said Geraint, "that thou wilt go to Gwenhwyvar, the wife of Arthur, to do her satisfaction for the insult which her maiden received from thy dwarf. As to myself, for the insult which I received from thee and thy dwarf, I am content with that which I have done unto thee. Dismount not from the time thou goest hence until thou comest into the presence of Gwenhwyvar, to make her what atonement shall be adjudged at the Court of Arthur." "This will I do gladly. And who art thou?" said he. "I am Geraint the son of Erbin. And declare thou also who thou art." "I am Edeyrn the son of Nudd." Then he threw himself upon his horse, and went forward to Arthur's Court, and the lady he loved best went before him and the dwarf, with much lamentation. And thus far this story up to that time.

Then came the little Earl and his hosts to Geraint, and saluted him, and bade him to his castle. "I may not go," said Geraint, "but where I was last night, there will I be to-night also." "Since thou wilt none of my inviting, thou shalt have abundance of all that I can command for thee, in the place thou wast last night. And I will order ointment for thee, to recover thee from thy fatigues, and from the weariness that is upon thee." "Heaven reward thee," said Geraint, "and I will go to my lodging." And thus went Geraint, and Earl Ynywl, and his wife, and his daughter. And when they reached the chamber, the household servants and attendants of the young Earl had arrived at the Court, and they arranged all the houses, dressing them with straw and with fire; and in a short time the ointment was ready, and Geraint came there, and they washed his head. Then came the young Earl, with forty honourable knights from among his attendants, and those who were bidden to the tournament. And Geraint came from the anointing. And the Earl asked him to go to the hall to eat. "Where is the Earl Ynywl," said Geraint, "and his wife, and his daughter?" "They are in the chamber yonder," said the Earl's chamberlain, "arraying themselves in garments which the Earl has caused to be brought for them." "Let not the damsel array herself," said he, "except in her vest and her veil, until she come to the Court of Arthur, to be clad by Gwenhwyvar, in such garments as she may choose." So the maiden did not array herself.

Then they all entered the hall, and they washed, and went, and sat down to meat. And thus were they seated. On one side of Geraint sat the young Earl, and Earl Ynywl beyond him; and on the other side of Geraint was the maiden and her mother. And after these all sat according to their precedence in honour. And they ate. And they were served abundantly, and they received a profusion of divers kind of gifts. Then they conversed together. And the young Earl invited Geraint to visit him next day. "I will not, by Heaven," said Geraint. "To the Court of Arthur will I go with this maiden to-morrow And it is enough for me, as long as Earl Ynywl is in

poverty and trouble ; and I go chiefly to seek to add
to his maintenance." " Ah, chieftain," said the young
Earl, "it is not by my fault that Earl Ynywl is without his possessions." "By my faith," said Geraint,
"he shall not remain without them, unless death
quickly takes me hence." " Oh, chieftain," said he,
"with regard to the disagreement, between me and
Ynywl, I will gladly abide by thy counsel, and agree
to what thou mayest judge right between us."[1] " I
but ask thee," said Geraint, "to restore to him what
is his, and what he should have received from the
time he lost his possessions, even until this day."
"That will I do gladly, for thee," answered he.
"Then," said Geraint, "whosoever is here who owes
homage to Ynywl, let him come forward, and perform
it on the spot." And all the men did so. And by
that treaty they abided. And his castle, and his
town, and all his possessions, were restored to Ynywl.
And he received back all that he had lost, even to the
smallest jewel.

Then spoke Earl Ynywl to Geraint. "Chieftain,"
said he "behold the maiden for whom thou didst
challenge at the tournament, I bestow her upon
thee." "She shall go with me," said Geraint, "to the
Court of Arthur ; and Arthur and Gwenhwyvar, they
shall dispose of her as they will." And the next day
they proceeded to Arthur's Court. So far concerning
Geraint.

Now, this 'is how Arthur hunted the stag. The
men and the dogs were divided into hunting parties,
and the dogs were let loose upon the stag. And the
last dog that was let loose was the favourite dog of

[1] As thou art impartial concerning the question of right
between us.

Arthur.   Cavall was his name.   And he left all the
other dogs behind him, and turned the stag.   And at
the second turn, the stag came towards the hunting
party of Arthur.   And Arthur set upon him.   And
before he could be slain by any other, Arthur cut off
his head.   Then they sounded the death horn for
slaying,.and they all gathered round.

Then came Kadyrieith to Arthur, and spoke to
him.   "Lord," said he, "behold yonder is Gwenhwyvar, and none with her save only one maiden."
"Command Gildas the son of Caw, and all the
scholars of the Court," said Arthur, "to attend
Gwenhwyvar to the palace."   And they did so.

Then they all set forth, holding converse together
concerning the head of the stag, to whom it should
be given.   One wished that it should be given to the
lady best beloved by him, and another to the lady
whom he loved best.   And all they of the household
and the knights disputed sharply concerning the head.
And with that they came to the palace.   And when
Arthur and Gwenhwyvar heard them disputing about
the head of the stag, Gwenhwyvar said to Arthur,
"My lord, this is my counsel concerning the stag's
head; let it not be given away until Geraint the son
of Erbin shall return from the errand he is upon."
And Gwenhwyvar told Arthur what that errand
was.   "Right gladly shall it be so," said Arthur.
And thus it was settled.   And the next day Gwenhwyvar caused a watch to be set upon the ramparts
for Geraint's coming.   And after mid-day they beheld
an unshapely little man upon a horse, and after him,
as they supposed, a dame or a damsel, also on horseback, and after her a knight of large stature, bowed
down, and hanging his head low and sorrowfully, and
clad in broken and worthless armour,

And before they came near to the gate, one of the watch went to Gwenhwyvar, and told her what kind of people they saw, and what aspect they bore. "I know not who they are," said he. "But I know," said Gwenhwyvar, "this is the knight whom Geraint pursued, and methinks that he comes not here by his own free will. But Geraint has overtaken him, and avenged the insult to the maiden to the uttermost." And thereupon, behold a porter came to the spot where Gwenhwyvar was. "Lady," said he, "at the gate there is a knight, and I saw never a man of so pitiful an aspect to look upon as he. Miserable and broken is the armour that he wears, and the hue of blood is more conspicuous upon it than its own colour." "Knowest thou his name?" said she. "I do," said he, "he tells me that he is Edeyrn the son of Nudd." Then she replied, "I know him not."

So Gwenhwyvar went to the gate to meet him, and he entered. And Gwenhwyvar was sorry when she saw the condition he was in, even though he was accompanied by the churlish dwarf. Then Edeyrn saluted Gwenhwyvar. "Heaven protect thee," said she. "Lady," said he, "Geraint the son of Erbin, thy best and most valiant servant, greets thee." "Did he meet with thee?" she asked. "Yes," said he, "and it was not to my advantage; and that was not his fault, but mine, Lady. And Geraint greets thee well; and in greeting thee he compelled me to come hither to do thy pleasure for the insult which thy maiden received from the dwarf. He forgives the insult to himself, in consideration of his having put me in peril of my life. And he imposed on me a condition, manly, and honourable, and warrior-like, which was to do thee justice, Lady." "Now, where did he overtake thee?" "At the place where we were

jousting, and contending for the Sparrow-Hawk, in
the town which is now called Cardiff. And there
were none with him, save three persons, of a mean
and tattered condition. And these were an aged,
hoary-headed man and a woman advanced in years,
and a fair young maiden, clad in worn-out garments.
And it was for the avouchment of the love of that
maiden that Geraint jousted for the Sparrow-Hawk at
the tournament; for he said that that maiden was
better entitled to the Sparrow-Hawk than this maiden
who was with me. And thereupon we encountered
each other, and he left me, Lady, as thou seest."
"Sir," said she, "when thinkest thou that Geraint
will be here?" "To-morrow, Lady, I think he will
be here with the maiden."

Then Arthur came to him, and he saluted Arthur,
and Arthur gazed a long time upon him, and was
amazed to see him thus. And thinking that he knew
him, he enquired of him, "Art thou Edeyrn the son
of Nudd?" "I am, Lord," said he, "and I have
met with much trouble, and received wounds un-
supportable." Then he told Arthur all his adventure.

"Well," said Arthur, "from what I hear, it behoves
Gwenhwyvar to be merciful towards thee." "The
mercy which thou desirest, Lord," said she, "will I
grant to him, since it is as insulting to thee that an
insult should be offered to me as to thyself." "Thus
will it be best to do," said Arthur, "let this man have
medical care until it be known whether he may live.
And if he live, he shall do such satisfaction as shall
be judged best by the men of the Court; and take
thou sureties to that effect. And if he die, too much
will be the death of such a youth as Edeyrn for an
insult to a maiden." "This pleases me," said
Gwenhwyvar. And Arthur became surety for Edeyrn,

and Caradawc the son of Llyr, Gwallawg the son of
Llenawg, and Owain the son of Nudd, and Gwalchmai,
and many others with them. And Arthur caused
Morgan Tud to be called to him. He was the chief
physician. "Take with thee Edeyrn the son of
Nudd, and cause a chamber to be prepared for him,
and let him have the aid of medicine as thou wouldest
do unto myself if I were wounded, and let none into
his chamber to molest him, but thyself and thy
disciples, to administer to him remedies." "I will
do so, gladly, Lord," said Morgan Tud. Then
said the steward of the household, "Whither is it
right, Lord, to order the maiden?" "To Gwenhwyvar and her handmaidens," said he. And the
Steward of the Household so ordered her. Thus far
concerning them.

The next day came Geraint towards the Court, and
there was a watch set on the ramparts by Gwenhwyvar,
lest he should arrive unawares. And one of the
watch came to the place where Gwenhwyvar was.
"Lady," said he, "methinks that I see Geraint, and
the maiden with him. He is on horseback, but he
has his walking gear upon him, and the maiden
appears to be in white, seeming to be clad in a garment of linen." "Assemble all the women," said
Gwenhwyvar, "and come to meet Geraint, to welcome
him, and wish him joy." And Gwenhwyvar went to
meet Geraint and the maiden. And when Geraint
came to the place where Gwenhwyvar was, he saluted
her. "Heaven prosper thee," said she, "and welcome to thee. And thy career has been successful,
and fortunate, and resistless, and glorious. And
Heaven reward thee, that thou hast so proudly caused
me to have retribution." "Lady," said he, "I

earnestly desired to obtain thee satisfaction according to thy will; and, behold, here is the maiden
through whom thou hadst thy revenge." "Verily,"
said Gwenhwyvar, "the welcome of Heaven be unto
her; and it is fitting that we should receive her
joyfully." Then they went in, and dismounted. And
Geraint came to where Arthur was, and saluted him.
"Heaven protect thee," said Arthur, "and the welcome of Heaven be unto thee. And since [1] Edeyrn
the son of Nudd has received his overthrow and
wounds from thy hands, thou hadst had a prosperous
career." "Not upon me be the blame," said Geraint,
"it was through the arrogance of Edeyrn the son of
Nudd himself that we were not friends. I would not
quit him until I knew who he was, and until the one
had vanquished the other." "Now," said Arthur,
"where is the maiden for whom I heard thou didst
give challenge?" "She is gone with Gwenhwyvar to
her chamber." Then went Arthur to see the maiden.
And Arthur, and all his companions, and his whole
Court, were glad concerning the maiden. And
certain were they all, that had her array been suitable
to her beauty, they had never seen a maid fairer than
she. And Arthur gave away the maiden to Geraint.
And the usual bond made between two persons was
made between Geraint and the maiden, and the
choicest of all Gwenhwyvar's apparel was given to the
maiden; and thus arrayed, she appeared comely and
graceful to all·who beheld her. And that.day and
that night were spent in abundance of minstrelsy,
and ample gifts of liquor, and a multitude of games.
And when it was time for them to go to sleep, they
went. And in the chamber where the couch of

---

[1] More probably "though." The ambiguity of the original
would be best expressed by "while."

Arthur and Gwenhwyvar was, the couch of Geraint
and Enid was prepared. And from that time she
became his bride. And the next day Arthur satisfied
all the claimants upon Geraint with bountiful gifts.
And the maiden took up her abode in the palace, and
she had many companions, both men and women,
and there was no maiden more esteemed than she in
the Island of Britain.

Then spake Gwenhwyvar. " Rightly did I judge,"
said she, "concerning the head of the stag, that it
should not be given to any until Geraint's return ;
and, behold, here is a fit occasion for bestowing it.
Let it be given to Enid, the daughter of Ynywl, the
most illustrious maiden. And I do not believe that
any will begrudge it her, for between her and every
one here there exists nothing but love and friendship."
Much applauded was this by them all, and by Arthur
also. And the head of the stag was given to Enid.
And thereupon her fame increased, and her friends
thenceforward became more in number than before.
And Geraint from that time forth loved the stag, and
the tournament, and hard encounters ; and he came
victorious from them all. And a year, and a second,
and a third, he proceeded thus, until his fame had
flown over the face of the kingdom.

And once upon a time, Arthur was holding his
Court at Caerlleon upon Usk, at Whitsuntide. And,
behold, there came to him ambassadors, wise and
prudent, full of knowledge, and eloquent of speech,
and they saluted Arthur. "Heaven prosper you,"
said Arthur, "and the welcome of Heaven be unto
you. And whence do you come?" "We come,
Lord," said they, "from Cornwall ; and we are
ambassadors from Erbin the son of Custennin, thy
uncle, and our mission is unto thee. And he greets

thee well, as an uncle should greet his nephew, and
as a vassal should greet his lord.   And he represents
unto thee that he waxes heavy and feeble, and is
advancing in years.   And the neighbouring chiefs
knowing this, grow insolent towards him, and covet
his land and possessions.   And he earnestly beseeches
thee, Lord, to permit Geraint his son to return to him,
to protect his possessions, and to become acquainted
with his boundaries.   And unto him he represents
that it were better for him to spend the flower of his
youth, and the prime of his age, in preserving his own
boundaries, than in tournaments, which are productive
of no profit, although he obtains glory in them."

"Well," said Arthur, " go, and divest yourselves of
your accoutrements, and take food, and refresh yourselves after your fatigues ; and before you go forth
hence you shall have an answer."   And they went to
eat.   And Arthur considered that it would go hard
with him to let Geraint depart from him and from his
Court ; neither did he think it fair that his cousin
should be restrained from going to protect his
dominions and his boundaries, seeing that his father
was unable to do so.   No less was the grief and
regret of Gwenhwyvar, and all her women, and all
her damsels, through fear that the maiden would
leave them.   And that day and that night were spent
in abundance of feasting.   And Arthur showed
Geraint the cause of the mission, and of the coming
of the ambassadors to him out of Cornwall.   " Truly,"
said Geraint, " be it to my advantage or disadvantage,
Lord, I will do according to thy will concerning this
embassy."   " Behold," said Arthur, " though it grieves
me to part with thee, it is my counsel that thou go to
dwell in thine own dominions, and to defend thy
boundaries, and to take with thee to accompany thee

as many as thou wilt of those thou lovest best among
my faithful ones, and among thy friends, and among
thy companions in arms." "Heaven reward thee;
and this will I do," said Geraint. "What discourse,"
said Gwenhwyvar, "do I hear between you? Is it
of those who are to conduct Geraint to his country?"
"It is," said Arthur. "Then is it needful for me to
consider," said she, "concerning companions and a
provision for the lady that is with me?" "Thou wilt
do well," said Arthur.

And that night they went to sleep. And the next
day the ambassadors were permitted to depart, and
they were told that Geraint should follow them. And
on the third day Geraint set forth, and many went
with him. Gwalchmai the son of Gwyar, and
Riogonedd the son of the king of Ireland, and
Ondyaw the son of the duke of Burgandy, Gwilim the
son of the ruler of the Franks, Howel the son of
Emyr of Brittany, Elivry, and Nawkyrd, Gwynn the
son of Tringad, Goreu the son of Custennin, Gweir
Gwrhyd Vawr, Garannaw the son of Golithmer,
Peredur the son of Evrawc, Gwynnllogell, Gwyr a
judge in the Court of Arthur, Dyvyr the son of Alun
of Dyved, Gwrei Gwalstawd Ieithoedd, Bedwyr the
son of Bedrawd, Hadwry the son of Gwryon, Kai the
son of Kynyr, Odyar the Frank, the Steward of
Arthur's Court, and Edeyrn the son of Nudd. Said
Geraint, " I think that I shall have enough of knighthood with me." " Yes," said Arthur, "but it will not
be fitting for thee to take Edeyrn with thee, although
he is well, until peace shall be made between him and
Gwenhwyvar." " Gwenhwyvar can permit him to go
with me, if he gives sureties." " If she please, she
can let him go without sureties, for enough of pain
and affliction has he suffered for the insult which the

maiden received from the dwarf." "Truly," said
Gwenhwyvar, "since it seems well to thee and to
Geraint, I will do this gladly, Lord." Then she
permitted Edeyrn freely to depart. And many there
were who accompanied Geraint, and they set forth ;
and never was there seen a fairer host journeying
towards the Severn. And on the other side of the
Severn were the nobles of Erbin the son of Custennin,
and his foster father at their head, to welcome Geraint
with gladness ; and many of the women of the Court,
with his mother, came to receive Enid the daughter
of Ynywl, his wife. And there was great rejoicing
and gladness throughout the whole Court, and
throughout all the country, concerning Geraint,
because of the greatness of their love towards him,
and of the greatness of the fame which he had gained
since he went from amongst them, and because he
was come to take possession of his dominions, and to
preserve his boundaries. And they came to the
Court. And in the Court they had ample entertainment, and a multitude of gifts, and abundance of
liquor, and a sufficiency of service, and a variety of
minstrelsy and of games. And to do honour to
Geraint, all the chief men of the country were invited
that night to visit him. And they passed that day
and that night in the utmost enjoyment. And at
dawn next day Erbin arose, and summoned to him
Geraint, and the noble persons who had borne him
company. And he said to Geraint, "I am a feeble
and an aged man, and whilst I was able to maintain
the dominion for thee and for myself, I did so. But
thou art young, and in the flower of thy vigour and of
thy youth : henceforth do thou preserve thy possessions." "Truly," said Geraint, "with my consent
thou shalt not give the power over thy dominions at

this time into my hands, and thou shalt not take me from Arthur's Court." "Into thy hands will I give them," said Erbin, "and this day also shalt thou receive the homage of thy subjects."

Then said Gwalchmai, "It were better for thee to satisfy those who have boons to ask, to-day, and to-morrow thou canst receive the homage of thy dominions." So all that had boons to ask were summoned into one place. And Kadyrieith came to them, to know what were their requests. And every one asked that which he desired. And the followers of Arthur began to make gifts and immediately the men of Cornwall came, and gave also. And they were not long in giving, so eager was every one to bestow gifts. And of those who came to ask gifts, none departed unsatisfied. And that day and that night were spent in the utmost enjoyment.

And the next day, at dawn, Erbin desired Geraint to send messengers to the men, to ask them whether it was displeasing to them that he should come to receive their homage, and whether they had anything to object to him. Then Geraint sent ambassadors to the men of Cornwall, to ask them this. And they all said that it would be the fulness of joy and honour to them for Geraint to come and receive their homage. So he received the homage of such as were there. And they remained with him till the third night. And the day after the followers of Arthur intended to go away. "It is too soon for you to go away yet," said he, "stay with me until I have finished receiving the homage of my chief men, who have agreed to come to me." And they remained with him until he had done so. Then they set forth towards the Court of Arthur; and Geraint went to bear them company, and Enid also, as far as Diganhwy: there they parted.

Then Ondyaw the son of the duke of Burgundy said to Geraint, "Go first of all, and visit the uttermost parts of thy dominions, and see well to the boundaries of thy territories; and if thou hast any trouble respecting them, send unto thy companions." "Heaven reward thee," said Geraint, "and this will I do." And Geraint journeyed to the uttermost part of his dominions. And experienced guides, and the chief men of his country, went with him. And the furthermost point that they showed him he kept possession of.

And, as he had been used to do when he was at Arthur's Court, he frequented tournaments. And he became acquainted with valiant and mighty men, until he had gained as much fame there as he had formerly done elsewhere. And he enriched his Court, and his companions, and his nobles, with the best horses, and the best arms, and with the best and most valuable jewels, and he ceased not until his fame had flown over the face of the whole kingdom. And when he knew that it was thus, he began to love ease and pleasure, for there was no one who was worth his opposing. And he loved his wife, and liked to continue in the palace, with minstrelsy and diversions. And for a long time he abode at home. And after that he began to shut himself up in the chamber of his wife, and he took no delight in anything besides, insomuch that he gave up the friendship of his nobles, together with his hunting and his amusements, and lost the hearts of all the host in his Court; and there was murmuring and scoffing concerning him among the inhabitants of the palace, on account of his relinquishing so completely their companionship for the love of his wife. And these tidings came to Erbin. And when Erbin had heard

C

these things, he spoke unto Enid, and enquired of
her whether it was she that had caused Geraint to
act thus, and to forsake his people and his hosts.
"Not I, by my confession unto Heaven," said she ;
"there is nothing more hateful to me than this."
And she knew not what she should do, for, although
it was hard for her to own this to Geraint, yet was it
not more easy for her to listen to what she heard
without warning Geraint concerning it. And she was
very sorrowful.

And one morning in the summer time, they were
upon their couch, and Geraint lay upon the edge of
it. And Enid was without sleep in the apartment,
which had windows of glass. And the sun shone
upon the couch. And the clothes had slipped from
off his arms and his breast, and he was asleep. Then
she gazed upon the marvellous beauty of his appearance, and she said, "Alas, and am I the cause that
these arms and this breast have lost their glory and
the warlike fame which they once so richly enjoyed ! "
And as she said this, the tears dropped from her eyes,
and they fell upon his breast. And the tears she
shed, and the words she had spoken, awoke him ;
and another thing contributed to awaken him, and
that was the idea that it was not in thinking of him
that she spoke thus, but that it was because she loved
some other man more than him, and that she wished
for other society, and thereupon Geraint was troubled
in his mind, and he called his squire ; and when he
came to him, "Go quickly," said he, "and prepare
my horse and my arms, and make them ready. And
do thou arise," said he to Enid, "and apparel thyself ;
and cause thy horse to be accoutred, and clothe thee
in the worst riding dress that thou hast in thy possession. And evil betide me," said he, "if thou return-

est here until thou knowest whether I have lost my
strength so completely as thou didst say. And if it
be so, it will then be easy for thee to seek the society
thou didst wish for of him of whom thou wast thinking." So she arose, and clothed herself in her
meanest garments. "I know nothing, Lord," said
she, "of thy meaning." "Neither wilt thou know at
this time," said he.

Then Geraint went to see Erbin. "Sir," said he,
"I am going upon a quest, and I am not certain
when I may come back. Take heed, therefore, unto
thy possessions, until my return." "I will do so,"
said he, "but it is strange to me that thou shouldst
go so suddenly. And who will proceed with thee,
since thou art not strong enough to traverse the land
of Lloegyr alone." "But one person only will go
with me." "Heaven counsel thee, my son," said
Erbin, "and may many attach themselves to thee in
Lloegyr." Then went Geraint to the place where his
horse was, and it was equipped with foreign armour,
heavy and shining. And he desired Enid to mount
her horse, and to ride forward, and to keep a long
way before him. "And whatever thou mayest see,
and whatever thou mayest hear, concerning me," said
he, "do thou not turn back. And unless I speak
unto thee, say not thou one word either." And they
set forward. And he did not choose the pleasantest
and most frequented road, but that which was the
wildest and most beset by thieves, and robbers, and
venomous animals. And they came to a high road,
which they followed till they saw a vast forest, and
they went towards it, and they saw four armed horsemen come forth from the forest. When they had
beheld them, one of them said to the other, "Behold,
here is a good occasion for us to capture two horses

and armour, and a lady likewise; for this we shall
have no difficulty in doing against yonder single
knight, who hangs his head so pensively and heavily."
And Enid heard this discourse, and she knew not
what she should do through fear of Geraint, who had
told her to be silent. "The vengeance of Heaven
be upon me," she said, "if I would not rather receive
my death from his hand than from the hand of any
other; and though he should slay me, yet will I speak
to him, lest I should have the misery to witness his
death."[1] So she waited for Geraint until he came
near to her. "Lord," said she, "didst thou hear
the words of those men concerning thee?" Then
he lifted up his eyes, and looked at her angrily.
"Thou hadst only," said he, "to hold thy peace as I
bade thee. I wish but for silence and not for warning.[2]
And though thou shouldst desire to see my defeat
and my death by the hands of those men, yet do I
feel no dread." Then the foremost of them couched
his lance, and rushed upon Geraint. And he received him, and that not feebly. But he let the
thrust go by him, while he struck the horseman upon
the centre of his shield in such a manner, that his
shield was split, and his armour broken, and so that
a cubit's length of the shaft of Geraint's lance passed
through his body, and sent him to the earth the
length of the lance over his horse's crupper. Then
the second horseman attacked him furiously, being
wroth at the death of his companion. But with one
thrust Geraint overthrew him also, and killed him as
he had done the other. Then the third set upon
him, and he killed him in like manner. And thus

[1] "Lest he should be overtaken by a piteous death."
[2] "Thine I do not consider a protection, nor thy warning a
warning."

also he slew the fourth. Sad and sorrowful was the
maiden as she saw all this. Geraint dismounted his
horse, and took the arms of the men he had slain,
and placed them upon their saddles, and tied
together the reins of their horses, and he mounted
his horse again. " Behold what thou must do," said.
he, " take the four horses, and drive them before thee,
and proceed forward, as I bade thee just now. And
say not one word unto me, unless I speak first unto
thee. And I declare unto Heaven," said he, " if
thou doest not thus, it will be to thy cost." " I will
do, as far as I can, Lord," said she, "according to
thy desire." Then they went forward through the
forest ; and when they left the forest, they came to a
vast plain, in the centre of which was a group of
thickly tangled copse-wood ; and from out thereof
they beheld three horsemen coming towards them,
well equipped with armour, both they and their
horses. Then the maiden looked steadfastly upon
them ; and when they had come near, she heard
them say one to another, "Behold, here is a good
arrival for us, here are coming for us four horses
and four suits of armour. We shall easily obtain
them spite of yonder dolorous knight, and the maiden
also will fall into our power." "This is but too
true," said she to herself, "for my husband is tired
with his former combat. The vengeance of Heaven
will be upon me, unless I warn him of this." So
the maiden waited until Geraint came up to her.
" Lord," said she, "dost thou not hear the discourse
of yonder men concerning thee ? " " What was it ? "
asked he. " They say to one another, that they will
easily obtain all this spoil." " I declare to Heaven,"
he answered, "that their words are less grievous to
me than that thou wilt not be silent, and abide by my

counsel." "My Lord," said she, "I feared lest they should surprise thee unawares." "Hold thy peace then," said he, "do not I desire silence?"[1] And thereupon one of the horsemen couched his lance, and attacked Geraint. And he made a thrust at him, which he thought would be very effective; but Geraint received it carelessly, and struck it aside, and then he rushed upon him, and aimed at the centre of his person, and from the shock of man and horse, the quantity of his armour did not avail him, and the head of the lance and part of the shaft passed through him, so that he was carried to the ground an arm and a spear's length over the crupper of his horse. And both the other horsemen came forward in their turn, but their onset was not more successful than that of their companion. And the maiden stood by, looking at all this; and on the one hand she was in trouble lest Geraint should be wounded in his encounter with the men, and on the other hand she was joyful to see him victorious. Then Geraint dismounted, and bound the three suits of armour upon the three saddles, and he fastened the reins of all the horses together, so that he had seven horses with him. And he mounted his own horse, and commanded the maiden to drive forward the others. "It is no more use for me to speak to thee than to refrain, for thou wilt not attend to my advice." "I will do so, as far I am able, Lord," said she; "but I cannot conceal from thee the fierce and threatening words which I may hear against thee, Lord, from such strange people as those that haunt this wilderness." "I declare to Heaven," said he, "that I desire nought but silence;

---

[1] "Wilt thou not at last be silent? Thy protection do I not consider such."

therefore, hold thy peace."[1]   "I will, Lord, while I
can." And the maiden went on with the horses
before her, and she pursued her way straight onwards.
And from the copse-wood already mentioned, they
journeyed over a vast and dreary open plain. And
at a great distance from them they beheld a wood,
and they could see neither end nor boundary to the
wood, except on that side that was nearest to them,
and they went towards it. Then there came from
out the wood five horsemen, eager, and bold, and
mighty, and strong, mounted upon chargers that were
powerful, and large of bone, and high-mettled, and
proudly snorting, and both the men and the horses
were well equipped with arms. And when they drew
near to them, Enid heard them say, " Behold, here is
a fine booty coming to us, which we shall obtain
easily and without labour, for we shall have no
trouble in taking all those horses and arms, and the
lady also, from yonder single knight, so doleful and
sad."

Sorely grieved was the maiden upon hearing this
discourse, so that she knew not in the world what she
should do. At last, however, she determined to warn
Geraint ; so she turned her horse's head towards him.
" Lord," said she, "if thou hadst heard as I did what
yonder horsemen said concerning thee, thy heaviness
would be greater than it is." Angrily and bitterly
did Geraint smile upon her, and he said, "Thee do
I hear doing everything that I forbade thee ; but it
may be that thou wilt repent this yet." And immediately, behold, the men met them, and victoriously
and gallantly did Geraint overcome them all five.
And he placed the five suits of armour upon the five

---

[1] " I declare to Heaven," said he, "that thy protection I do
not regard as such. Hold thy peace, at last."

saddles, and tied together the reins of the twelve
horses, and gave them in charge to Enid. "I know
not," said he, "what good it is for me to order thee:
but this time I charge thee in an especial manner."
So the maiden went forward towards the wood,
keeping in advance of Geraint, as he had desired
her; and it grieved him as much as his wrath would
permit, to see a maiden so illustrious as she having
so much trouble with the care of the horses. Then
they reached the wood, and it was both deep and
vast; and in the wood night overtook them. "Ah,
maiden," said he, "it is vain to attempt proceeding
forward!" "Well, Lord," said she, "whatsoever thou
wishest, we will do." "It will be best for us," he
answered, "to turn out of the wood, and to rest, and
wait for the day, in order to pursue our journey."
"That will we, gladly," said she. And they did so.
Having dismounted himself, he took her down from
her horse. "I cannot, by any means, refrain from
sleep, through weariness," said he. "Do thou, therefore, watch the horses, and sleep not." "I will,
Lord," said she. Then he went to sleep in his
armour, and thus passed the night, which was not
long at that season. And when she saw the dawn of
day appear, she looked around her, to see if he were
waking, and thereupon he woke. "My Lord," she
said, "I have desired to awake thee for some time."
But he spake nothing to her about fatigue,[1] as he had
desired her to be silent. Then he arose, and said
unto her, "Take the horses, and ride on; and keep
straight on before thee as thou didst yesterday."
And early in the day they left the wood, and they
came to an open country, with meadows on one hand,
and mowers mowing the meadows. And there was a

---

[1] He spoke not a word, being angry.

river before them, and the horses bent down, and drank the water. And they went up out of the river by a lofty steep; and there they met a slender stripling, with a satchel about his neck, and they saw that there was something in the satchel, but they knew not what it was. And he had a small blue pitcher in his hand, and a bowl on the mouth of the pitcher. And the youth saluted Geraint. "Heaven prosper thee," said Geraint, "and whence dost thou come?" "I come," said he, "from the city that lies before thee. My Lord," he added, "will it be displeasing to thee, if I ask whence thou comest also?" "By no means—through yonder wood did I come." "Thou camest not through the wood to-day." "No," he replied, "we were in the wood last night." "I warrant," said the youth, "that thy condition there last night was not the most pleasant, and that thou hadst neither meat nor drink." "No, by my faith," said he. "Wilt thou follow my counsel," said the youth, "and take thy meal from me?" "What sort of meal?" he enquired. "The breakfast which is sent for yonder mowers, nothing less than bread and meat, and wine; and if thou wilt, Sir, they shall have none of it." "I will," said he, "and Heaven reward thee for it."

So Geraint alighted, and the youth took the maiden from off her horse. Then they washed, and took their repast. And the youth cut the bread in slices, and gave them drink, and served them withal. And when they had finished, the youth arose, and said to Geraint, "My Lord, with thy permission I will now go and fetch some food for the mowers." "Go, first, to the town," said Geraint, "and take a lodging for me in the best place that thou knowest, and the most commodious one for the horses, and take thou

whichever horse and arms thou choosest in pay-
ment for thy service and thy gift." "Heaven reward
thee, Lord," said the youth, "and this would be
ample to repay services much greater than those I
rendered unto thee." And to the town went the
youth, and he took the best and the most pleasant
lodgings that he knew; and after that he went to the
palace, having the horse and armour with him, and
proceeded to the place where the Earl was, and told
him all his adventure. "I go now, Lord," said he,
"to meet the young man, and to conduct him to his
lodging." "Go gladly," said the Earl, "and right
joyfully shall he be received here, if he so come."
And the youth went to meet Geraint, and told him
that he would be received gladly by the Earl in his
own palace; but he would go only to his lodgings.
And he had a goodly chamber, in which was plenty
of straw, and draperies, and a spacious and commodious place he had for the horses, and the youth
prepared for them plenty of provender. · And after
they had disarrayed themselves, Geraint spoke thus to
Enid : "Go," said he, "to the other side of the
chamber, and come not to this side of the house;
and thou mayest call to thee the woman of the house,
if thou wilt." "I will do, Lord," said she, "as thou
sayest." And thereupon the man of the house came
to Geraint, and welcomed him. "Oh, chieftain,"
he said, "hast thou taken thy meal?" "I have,"
said he. Then the youth spoke to him, and enquired
if he would not drink something before he met the
Earl. "Truly, I will," said he. So the youth went
into the town, and brought them drink. And they
drank. "I must needs sleep," said Geraint. "Well,"
said the youth, "and whilst thou sleepest, I will go to
see the Earl." "Go, gladly," he said, "and come

here again when I require thee." And Geraint went to sleep, and so did Enid also.

And the youth came to the place where the Earl was, and the Earl asked him where the lodgings of the knight were, and he told him. "I must go," said the youth, "to wait on him in the evening." "Go," answered the Earl, "and greet him well from me, and tell him that in the evening I will go to see him." "This will I do," said the youth. So he came when it was time for them to awake. And they arose, and went forth. And when it was time for them to take their food they took it. And the youth served them. And Geraint enquired of the man of the house, whether there were any of his companions that he wished to invite to him, and he said that there were. "Bring them hither, and entertain them at my cost with the best thou canst buy in the town."

And the man of the house brought there those whom he chose, and feasted them at Geraint's expense. Thereupon, behold, the Earl came to visit Geraint, and his twelve honourable knights with him. And Geraint rose up, and welcomed him. "Heaven preserve thee," said the Earl. Then they all sat down according to their precedence in honour. And the Earl conversed with Geraint and enquired of him the object of his journey. "I have none," he replied, "but to seek adventures, and to follow my own inclination." Then the Earl cast his eye upon Enid, and he looked at her steadfastly. And he thought he had never seen a maiden fairer or more comely than she. And he set all his thoughts and his affections upon her. Then he asked of Geraint, "Have I thy permission to go and converse with yonder maiden, for I see that she is apart from thee?" "Thou hast it, gladly," said he. So the

Earl went to the place where the maiden was, and
spake with her. "Ah, maiden," said he, "it cannot
be pleasant to thee to journey thus with yonder
man!" "It is not unpleasant to me," said she, "to
journey the same road that he journeys." "Thou
hast neither youths nor maidens to serve thee," said
he. "Truly," she replied, "it is more pleasant for
me to follow yonder man than to be served by youths
and maidens." "I will give thee good counsel," said
he. "All my Earldom will I place in thy possession,
if thou wilt dwell with me." "That will I not, by
Heaven," she said, "yonder man was the first to
whom my faith was ever pledged; and shall I prove
inconstant to him?" "Thou art in the wrong," said
the Earl; "if I slay the man yonder, I can keep thee
with me as long as I choose; and when thou no
longer pleasest me, I can turn thee away. But if
thou goest with me by thy own good will, I protest
that our union shall continue eternal and undivided as
long as I remain alive." Then she pondered these
words of his, and she considered that it was advis
able to encourage him in his request. "Behold,
then, chieftain, this is most expedient for thee to do
to save me any needless imputation; come here to-
morrow, and take me away as though I knew nothing
thereof." "I will do so," said he. So he arose, and
took his leave, and went forth with his attendants.
And she told not then to Geraint any of the con-
versation which she had had with the Earl, lest it
should rouse his anger, and cause him uneasiness
and care.

And at the usual hour they went to sleep. And
at the beginning of the night Enid slept a little; and
at midnight she arose, and placed all Geraint's armour
together, so that it might be ready to put on. And

although fearful of her errand, she came to the side
of Geraint's bed; and she spoke to him softly and
gently, saying, "My Lord, arise, and clothe thyself,
for these were the words of the Earl to me, and his
intention concerning me." So she told Geraint all
that had passed. And although he was wroth with
her, he took warning, and clothed himself. And she
lighted a candle, that he might have light to do so.
"Leave there the candle," said he, "and desire the
man of the house to come here." Then she went,
and the man of the house came to him. "Dost thou
know how much I owe thee?" asked Geraint. "I
think thou owest but little." "Take the eleven
horses and the eleven suits of armour." "Heaven
reward thee, Lord," said he, "but I spent not the
value of one suit of armour upon thee." "For that
reason," said he, "thou wilt be the richer. And now
wilt thou come to guide me out of the town?" "I
will, gladly," said he, "and in which direction dost
thou intend to go?" "I wish to leave the town by a
different way from that by which I entered it." So
the man of the lodgings accompanied him as far as
he desired. Then he bade the maiden to go on
before him; and she did so, and went straight
forward, and his host returned home. And he had
only just reached his house, when, behold, the
greatest tumult approached that was ever heard.
And when he looked out he saw fourscore knights in
complete armour around the house, with the Earl
Dwrm at their head. "Where is the knight that
was here?" said the Earl. "By thy hand," said he,
"he went hence some time ago." "Wherefore,
villain," said he, "didst thou let him go without
informing me?" "My Lord, thou didst not command
me to do so, else would I not have allowed him to

depart." " What way dost thou think that he took ?."
" I know not, except that he went along the high
road." And they turned their horses' heads that
way, and seeing the tracks of the horses upon the
high road, they followed. And when the maiden
beheld the dawning of the day, she looked behind
her, and saw vast clouds of dust coming nearer and
nearer to her. And thereupon she became uneasy, :
and she thought that it was the Earl and his host
coming after them. And thereupon she beheld a
knight appearing through the mist. " By my faith,"
said she, "though he should slay me, it were better
for me to receive my death at his hands, than to see
him killed without warning him." " My Lord," she
said to him, " seest thou yonder man hastening after
thee, and many others with him ? " " I do see him,"
said he, "and in despite of all my orders, I see that
thou wilt never keep silence." Then he turned upon
the knight, and with the first thrust he threw him
down under his horse's feet. And as long as thère
remained one of the fourscore knights, he overthrew
every one of them at the first onset. And from the
weakest to the strongest, they all attacked him one
after the other, except the Earl : and last of all the
Earl came against him also. And he broke his lance,
and then he broke a second. But Geraint turned
upon him, and struck him with his lance upon the
centre of his shield, so that by that single thrust the
shield was split, and all his armour broken, and he
himself was brought over his horse's crupper to the
ground, and was in peril of his life. And Geraint
drew near to him ; and at the noise of the trampling
of his horse the Earl revived. " Mercy, Lord," said
he. to Geraint. And Geraint granted him mercy.
But through the hardness of the ground where they

had fallen, and the violence of the stroke which they
had received, there was not a single knight amongst
them that escaped without receiving a fall, mortally
severe, and grievously painful, and desperately wound-
ing, from the hand of Geraint.

And Geraint journeyed along the high road that
was before him, and the maiden went on first;
and near them they beheld a valley which was the
fairest ever seen, and which had a large river running
through it; and there was a bridge over the river, and
the high road led to the bridge. And above the
bridge, upon the opposite side of the river, they
beheld a fortified town, the fairest ever seen. And
as they approached the bridge, Geraint saw coming
towards him from a thick copse a man mounted upon
a large and lofty steed, even of pace and spirited
though tractable. "Ah, knight," said Geraint,
"whence comest thou?" "I come," said he "from
the valley below us." "Canst thou tell me," said
Geraint, "who is the owner of this fair valley and
yonder walled town?" "I will tell thee, willingly,"
said he, "Gwiffert Petit he is called by the Franks,
but the Welsh call him the Little King." "Can I go
by yonder bridge," said Geraint, "and by the lower
highway that is beneath the town?" Said the knight,
"Thou canst not go by his tower[1] on the other side of
the bridge, unless thou dost intend to combat him;
because it is his custom to encounter every knight
that comes upon his lands." "I declare to Heaven,"
said Geraint, "that I will, nevertheless, pursue my
journey that way."[2] "If thou dost so," said the
knight, "thou wilt probably meet with shame and

---

[1] "Do thou not go to his land beyond the bridge."
[2] "I will go my way in spite of the one thou speakest of."

disgrace in reward for thy daring."[1] Then Geraint
proceeded along the road that led to the town, and
the road brought him to a ground that was hard, and
rugged, and high, and ridgy.[2] And as he journeyed
thus, he beheld a knight following him upon a war-
horse, strong, and large, and proudly-stepping, and
wide-hoofed, and broad-chested. And he never saw
a man of smaller stature than he who was upon the
horse. And both he and his horse were completely
armed. When he had overtaken Geraint he said to

him, "Tell me, chieftain, whether it is through
ignorance or through presumption that thou seekest
to insult my dignity, and to infringe my rules?"
"Nay," answered Geraint, "I knew not that this road
was forbid to any." "Thou didst know it," said the
other; "come with me to my Court, to do me satisfaction." "That will I not, by my faith," said

[1] In a very rough and bitter manner.
[2] Gereint took the road that he had meant to take; it was
not the road that led to the town from the bridge that he took;
but the road that led to the ground that was hard, and rugged,
and high, and ridgy.

Geraint; "I would not go even to thy Lord's Court, excepting Arthur were thy Lord." "By the hand of Arthur himself," said the knight, "I will have satisfaction of thee, or receive my overthrow at thy hands." And immediately they charged one another. And a squire of his came to serve him with lances as he broke them. And they gave each other such hard and severe strokes, that their shields lost all their colour. But it was very difficult for Geraint to fight with him on account of his small size, for he was hardly able to get a full aim at him with all the efforts he could make.[1] And they fought thus until their horses were brought down upon their knees; and at length Geraint threw the knight headlong to the ground; and then they fought on foot, and they gave one another blows so boldly fierce, so frequent, and so severely powerful, that their helmets were pierced, and their skullcaps were broken, and their arms were shattered, and the light of their eyes was darkened by sweat and blood. At the last Geraint became enraged, and he called to him all his strength; and boldly angry, and swiftly resolute, and furiously determined, he lifted up his sword, and struck him on the crown of his head a blow so mortally painful, so violent, so fierce, and so penetrating, that it cut through all his head armour, and his skin, and his flesh, until it wounded the very bone, and the sword flew out of the hand of the Little King to the furthest end of the plain, and he besought Geraint that he would have mercy and compassion upon him. "Though thou hast been neither courteous nor just,"

---

[1] But it was unfair for Gereint to have to fight him, so small was he, and so difficult to take aim at, and so hard were the blows he gave. And they did not end that part of their fight until their horses fell down on their knees.

said Geraint, "thou shalt have mercy, upon condition that thou wilt become my ally, and engage never to fight against me again, but to come to my assistance whenever thou hearest of my being in trouble." "This will I do, gladly, Lord," said he. So he pledged him his faith thereof. "And now, Lord, come with me," said he, "to my Court yonder, to recover from thy weariness and fatigue." "That will I not, by Heaven," said he.

Then Gwiffert Petit beheld Enid where she stood, and it grieved him to see one of her noble mien appear so deeply afflicted. And he said to Geraint, "My Lord, thou doest wrong not to take repose, and refresh thyself awhile; for, if thou meetest with any difficulty in thy present condition, it will not be easy for thee to surmount it." But Geraint would do no other than proceed on his journey, and he mounted his horse in pain, and all covered with blood. And the maiden went on first, and they proceeded towards the wood which they saw before them.

And the heat of the sun was very great, and through the blood and sweat, Geraint's armour cleaved to his flesh; and when they came into the wood, he stood under a tree, to avoid the sun's heat; and his wounds pained him more than they had done at the time when he received them. And the maiden stood under another tree. And, lo! they heard the sound of horns, and a tumultuous noise, and the occasion of it was, that Arthur and his company had come down to the wood. And while Geraint was considering which way he should go to avoid them, behold, he was espied by a foot page, who was an attendant on the Steward of the Household, and he went to the steward, and told him what kind of man he had seen in the wood. Then the steward caused his horse to be saddled, and he took his lance and his shield, and went to the place where Geraint was. "Ah, knight!" said he, "what dost thou here?" "I am standing under a shady tree, to avoid the heat and the rays of the sun." "Wherefore is thy journey, and who art thou?" "I seek adventures, and go where I list." "Indeed," said Kai, "then come with me to see Arthur, who is here hard by." "That will I not, by Heaven," said Geraint. "Thou must needs come," said Kai. Then Geraint knew who he was, but Kai did not know Geraint. And Kai attacked Geraint as best as he could. And Geraint became wroth, and he struck him with the shaft of his lance, so that he rolled headlong to the ground. But chastisement worse than this would he not inflict on him.

Scared and wildly Kai arose, and he mounted his horse, and went back to his lodging. And thence he proceeded to Gwalchmai's tent. "Oh, Sir," said he to Gwalchmai, "I was told by one of the attendants, that he saw in the wood above a wounded knight, having on battered armour, and if thou dost right, thou wilt go and see if this be true." "I care not if I do so," said Gwalchmai. "Take, then, thy horse, and some of thy armour," said Kai, "for I hear that he is not over-courteous to those who approach him." So Gwalchmai took his spear and his shield, and mounted his horse, and came to the spot where Geraint was. "Sir Knight," said he, "wherefore is thy journey?" "I journey for my own pleasure, and to seek the adventures of the world." "Wilt thou tell me who thou art, or wilt thou come and visit Arthur, who is near at hand?" "I will make no alliance with thee, nor will I go and visit Arthur," said he. And he knew that it was Gwalchmai, but Gwalchmai knew him not. "I

purpose not to leave thee," said Gwalchmai, "till I
know who thou art." And he charged him with his
lance, and struck him on his shield, so that the shaft
was shivered into splinters, and their horses were
front to front. Then Gwalchmai gazed fixedly upon
him, and he knew him. " Ah, Geraint," said he, " is
it thou that art here ? " " I am not Geraint," said he.
"Geraint thou art, by Heaven," he replied, "and
a wretched and insane expedition is this." Then he
looked around, and beheld Enid, and he welcomed
her gladly. " Geraint," said Gwalchmai, ."come thou,
and see Arthur ; he is thy lord and thy cousin." " I
will not," said he, "for I am not in a fit state to go
and see any one." Thereupon, behold, one of the
pages came after Gwalchmai, to speak to him. So he
sent him to apprise Arthur that Geraint was there
wounded, and that he would not go to visit him, and
that it was pitiable to see the plight that he was in.
And this he did without Geraint's knowledge, inasmuch as he spoke in a whisper to the page. " Entreat
Arthur," said he, "to have his tent brought near to
the road, for he will not meet him willingly, and it is
not easy to compel him in the mood he is in." So
the page came to Arthur, and told him this. And he
caused his tent to be removed unto the side of the
road. And the maiden rejoiced in her heart. And
Gwalchmai led Geraint onwards along the road, till
they came to the place where Arthur was encamped,
and the pages were pitching his tent by the road-side.
"Lord," said Geraint, "all hail unto thee." " Heaven
prosper thee ; and who art thou ? " said Arthur.
" It is Geraint," said Gwalchmai, "and of his own
free will would he not come to meet thee." " Verily,"
said Arthur, " he is bereft of his reason." Then came
Enid, and saluted Arthur. " Heaven protect thee,'

said he. And thereupon he caused one of the pages to take her from her horse. "Alas! Enid," said Arthur, "what expedition is this?" "I know not, Lord," said she, "save that it behoves me to journey by the same road that he journeys." "My Lord," said Geraint, "with thy permission we will depart." "Whither wilt thou go?" said Arthur. "Thou canst not proceed now, unless it be unto thy death."[1] "He will not suffer himself to be invited by me," said Gwalchmai. "But by me he will," said Arthur; "and, moreover, he does not go from here until he is healed." "I had rather, Lord," said Geraint, "that thou wouldest let me go forth." "That will I not, I declare to Heaven," said he. Then he caused a maiden to be sent for to conduct Enid to the tent where Gwenhwyvar's chamber was. And Gwenhwyvar and all her women were joyful at her coming, and they took off her riding dress, and placed other garments upon her. Arthur also called Kadyrieith, and ordered him to pitch a tent for Geraint, and the physicians, and he enjoined him to provide him with abundance of all that might be requisite for him. And Kadyrieith did as he had commanded him. And Morgan Tud and his disciples were brought to Geraint.

And Arthur and his hosts remained there nearly a month, whilst Geraint was being healed. And when he was fully recovered, Geraint came to Arthur, and asked his permission to depart. "I know not if thou art quite well." "In truth I am, Lord," said Geraint. "I shall not believe thee concerning that, but the physicians that were with thee." So Arthur caused the physicians to be summoned to him, and asked them if it were true. "It is true, Lord," said Morgan

[1] "To complete thy death."

Tud. So the next day Arthur permitted him to go
forth, and he pursued his journey. And on the same
day Arthur removed thence. And Geraint desired
Enid to go on, and to keep before him, as she had
formerly done. And she went forward along the high
road. And as they journeyed thus, they heard an
exceeding loud wailing near to them. "Stay thou
here," said he, "and I will go and see what is the
cause of this wailing." " I will." said she. Then he
went forward into an open glade that was near the
road. And in the glade he saw two horses, one
having a man's saddle, and the other a woman's
saddle upon it. And, behold, there was a knight
lying dead in his armour, and a young damsel in a
riding dress standing over him, lamenting. "Ah!
Lady," said Geraint, "what hath befallen thee?"
"Behold," she answered, "I journeyed here with my
beloved husband, when, lo! three giants came upon
us, and without any cause in the world, they slew
him." "Which way went they hence?" said Geraint.
"Yonder by the high road," she replied. So he
returned to Enid. "Go," said he, "to the lady that
is below yonder, and await me there till I come."
She was sad when he ordered her to do thus, but
nevertheless she went to the damsel, whom it was
ruth to hear, and she felt certain that Geraint would
never return. Meanwhile Geraint followed the giants,
and overtook them. And each of them was greater
of stature than three other men, and a huge club was
on the shoulder of each. Then he rushed upon one
of them, and thrust his lance through his body. And
having drawn it forth again, he pierced another of them
through likewise. But the third turned upon him, and
struck him with his club, so that he split his shield,
and crushed his shoulder, and opened his wounds

anew, and all his blood began to flow from him. But
Geraint drew his sword, and attacked the giant, and
gave him a blow on the crown of his head so severe,
and fierce, and violent, that his head and his neck
were split down to his shoulders, and he fell dead.
So Geraint left him thus, and returned to Enid. And
when he saw her, he fell down lifeless from his horse.
Piercing, and loud, and thrilling was the cry that
Enid uttered. And she came and stood over him
where he had fallen. And at the sound of her cries
came the Earl of Limours, and the host that journeyed
with him, whom her lamentations brought out of
their road. And the Earl said to Enid, "Alas, Lady,
what hath befallen thee?" "Ah! good Sir," said
she, "the only man I have loved, or ever shall love,
is slain." Then he said to the other, "And what is
the cause of thy grief?" "They have slain my
beloved husband also," said she. "And who was it
that slew them?" "Some giants," she answered,
"slew my best beloved, and the other knight went in
pursuit of them, and came back in the state thou
seest, his blood flowing excessively; but it appears to
me that he did not leave the giants without killing some
of them, if not all." The Earl caused the knight
that was dead to be buried, but he thought that there
still remained some life in Geraint; and to see if he
yet would live, he had him carried with him in the
hollow of his shield, and upon a bier. And the two
damsels went to the court; and when they arrived
there, Geraint was placed upon a litter-couch in front
of the table that was in the hall. Then they all took
off their travelling gear, and the Earl besought Enid
to do the same, and to clothe herself in other garments. "I will not, by Heaven," said she. "Ah!
Lady," said he, "be not so sorrowful for this matter."

"It were hard to persuade me to be otherwise," said she. "I will act towards thee in such wise, that thou needest not be sorrowful, whether yonder knight live or die. Behold, a good Earldom, together with myself, will I bestow on thee; be, therefore, happy and joyful." "I declare to Heaven," said she, "that henceforth I shall never be joyful while I live." "Come, then," said he, "and eat." "No, by Heaven, I will not," she answered. "But by Heaven thou shalt," said he. So he took her with him to the table against her will, and many times desired her to eat. "I call Heaven to witness," said she, "that I will not eat until the man that is upon yonder bier shall eat likewise." "Thou canst not fulfil that," said the Earl, "yonder man is dead already." "I will prove that I can," said she. Then he offered her a goblet of liquor. "Drink this goblet," he said, "and it will cause thee to change thy mind." "Evil betide me," she answered, "if I drink aught until he drink also." "Truly," said the Earl, "it is of no more avail for me to be gentle with thee than ungentle." And he gave her a box in the ear. Thereupon she raised a loud and piercing shriek, and her lamentations were much greater than they had been before, for she considered in her mind that had Geraint been alive, he durst not have struck her thus. But, behold, at the sound of her cry Geraint revived from his swoon, and he sat up on the bier, and finding his sword in the hollow of his shield, he rushed to the place where the Earl was, and struck him a fiercely-wounding, severely-venomous, and sternly-smiting blow upon the crown of his head, so that he clove him in twain, until his sword was stayed by the table. Then all left the board and fled away. And this was not so much through fear of the living as through the dread they felt at seeing the dead man rise up to slay them. And Geraint looked upon Enid, and he was grieved for two causes; one was, to see that Enid had lost her colour and her wonted aspect; and the other, to know that she was in the right. "Lady," said he, "knowest thou where our horses are?" "I know, Lord, where thy horse is," she replied, "but I know not where is the other. Thy horse is in the house yonder." So he went to the house, and brought forth his horse, and mounted him, and took up Enid from the ground, and placed her upon the horse with him. And he rode forward. And their road lay between two hedges. And the night was gaining on the day. And, lo! they saw behind them the shafts of spears betwixt them and the sky, and they heard the trampling of horses, and the noise of a host approaching. "I hear something following us," said he, "and I will put thee on the other side of the hedge." And thus he did. And thereupon, behold, a knight pricked towards him, and couched his lance. When Enid saw this, she cried out, saying, "Oh! chieftain, whoever thou art, what renown wilt thou gain by slaying a dead man?" "Oh! Heaven," said he, "is it Geraint?" "Yes, in truth," said she. "And who art thou?" "I am the Little King," he answered, "coming to thy assistance, for I heard that thou wast in trouble. And if thou hadst followed my advice, none of these hardships would have befallen thee." "Nothing can happen," said Geraint, "without the will of Heaven, though much good results from counsel." "Yes," said the Little King, "and I know good counsel for thee now. Come with me to the court of a son-in-law of my sister, which is near here, and thou shalt have the best medical assistance in the kingdom." "I will do so,

gladly," said Geraint. And Enid was placed upon
the horse of one of the Little King's squires, and they
went forward to the Baron's palace. And they were
received there with gladness, and they met with
hospitality and attention. And the next morning they went to seek physicians; and it was not
long before they came, and they attended Geraint
until he was perfectly well. And while Geraint was
under medical care, the Little King caused his armour
to be repaired, until it was as good as it had ever
been. And they remained there a fortnight and a
month.

Then the Little King said to Geraint, "Now will
we go towards my own Court, to take rest and amuse
ourselves." "Not so," said Geraint, "we will first
journey for one day more, and return again." "With
all my heart," said the Little King, "do thou go
then." And early in the day they set forth. And
more gladly and more joyfully did Enid journey with
them that day than she had ever done. And they
came to the main road. And when they reached a
place where the road divided in two, they beheld a
man on foot coming towards them along one of these
roads, and Gwiffert asked the man whence he came.
"I come," said he, "from an errand in the country."
"Tell me," said Geraint, "which is the best for me
to follow of these two roads?" "That is the best for
thee to follow," answered he, "for if thou goest by
this one, thou wilt never return. Below us," said he,
there is a hedge of mist, and within it are enchanted
games, and no one who has gone there has ever returned. And the Court of the Earl Owain is there,
and he permits no one to go to lodge in the town
except he will go to his Court." "I declare to
Heaven," said Geraint, "that we will take the lower

road." And they went along it until they came to
the town. And they took the fairest and pleasantest
place in the town for their lodging. And while they
were thus, behold, a young man came to them, and
greeted them. "Heaven be propitious to thee," said
they. "Good Sirs," said he, "what preparations are
you making here?". "We are taking up our lodging,"
said they, "to pass the night." "It is not the custom
with him who owns the town," he answered, "to
permit any of gentle birth, unless they come to stay
in his Court, to abide here; therefore, come you to
the Court." "We will come, gladly," said Geraint.
And they went with the page, and they were joyfully
received. And the Earl came to the hall to meet
them, and he commanded the tables to be laid. And
they washed, and sat down. And this is the order in
which they sat, Geraint on one side of the Earl,
and Enid on the other side, and next to Enid the
Little King, and then the Countess next to Geraint,
and all after that as became their rank. Then
Geraint recollected the games, and thought that
he should not go to them; and on that account he
did not eat. Then the Earl looked upon Geraint,
and considered, and he bethought him that his not
eating was because of the games, and it grieved him
that he had ever established those games, were it only
on account of losing such a youth as Geraint. And
if Geraint had asked him to abolish the games, he
would gladly have done so. Then the Earl said to
Geraint, "What thought occupies thy mind, that thou
dost not eat? If thou hesitatest about going to the
games, thou shalt not go, and no other of thy rank
shall ever go either." "Heaven reward thee," said
Geraint, "but I wish nothing better than to go to the
games, and to be shown the way thither." "If that

is what thou dost prefer, thou shalt obtain it
willingly." "I do prefer it, indeed," said he. Then
they ate, and they were amply served, and they had a
variety of gifts, and abundance of liquor. And when
they had finished eating, they arose. And Geraint
called for his horse and his armour, and he accoutred
both himself and his horse. And all the hosts went
forth until they came to the side of the hedge, and
the hedge was so lofty, that it reached as high as
they could see in the air, and upon every stake in the
hedge, except two, there was the head of a man, and
the number of stakes throughout the hedge was very
great. Then said the Little King, "May no one go
in with the chieftain?" "No one may," said Earl
Owain. "Which way can I enter?" enquired
Geraint. "I know not," said Owain, "but enter by
the way that thou wilt, and that seemeth easiest to
thee."

Then fearlessly and unhesitatingly Geraint dashed
forward into the mist. And on leaving the mist he
came to a large orchard, and in the orchard he saw
an open space, wherein was a tent of red satin, and the
door of the tent was open, and an apple-tree stood
in front of the door of the tent, and on a branch of
the apple-tree hung a huge hunting horn. Then he
dismounted, and went into the tent, and there was
no one in the tent save one maiden sitting in a
golden chair, and another chair was opposite to her,
empty. And Geraint went to the empty chair, and
sat down therein. "Ah! chieftain," said the maiden,
"I would not counsel thee to sit in that chair."
"Wherefore?" said Geraint. "The man to whom
that chair belongs has never suffered another to sit
in it." "I care not," said Geraint, "though it dis-
please him that I sit in the chair." And thereupon

they heard a mighty tumult around the tent. And
Geraint looked to see what was the cause of the
tumult. And he beheld without a knight mounted
upon a war-horse, proudly-snorting, high-mettled, and
large of bone, and a robe of honour in two parts was
upon him and upon his horse, and beneath it was
plenty of armour. "Tell me, chieftain," said he to
Geraint, "who it was that bade thee sit there?"
"Myself," answered he. "It was wrong of thee to
do me this shame and disgrace. Arise, and do me
satisfaction for thine insolence.". Then Geraint arose,
and they encountered immediately, and they broke
a set of lances; and a second set; and a third; and
they gave each other fierce and frequent strokes;
and at last Geraint became enraged, and he urged
on his horse, and rushed upon him, and gave him a
thrust on the centre of his shield, so that it was split,
and so that the head of his lance went through his
armour, and his girths were broken, and he himself
was borne headlong to the ground the length of
Geraint's lance and arm, over his horse's crupper.
"Oh, my Lord!" said he, "thy mercy, and thou
shalt have what thou wilt." "I only desire," said
Geraint, "that this game shall no longer exist here,
nor the hedge of mist, nor magic, nor enchantment."
"Thou shalt have this gladly, Lord," he replied.
"Cause then the mist to disappear from this place,"
said Geraint. "Sound yonder horn," said he, "and
when thou soundest it, the mist will vanish; but it
will not go hence unless the horn be blown by the
knight by whom I am vanquished." And sad
and sorrowful was Enid where she remained, through
anxiety concerning Geraint. Then Geraint went and
sounded the horn. And at the first blast he gave,
the mist vanished. And all the hosts came together,

and they all became reconciled to each other. And the Earl invited Geraint and the Little King to stay with him that night. And the next morning they separated. And Geraint went towards his own dominions; and thenceforth he reigned prosperously, and his warlike fame and splendour lasted with renown and honour both to him and to Enid from that time forward.

THE DREAM OF MAXEN WLEDIG.

MAXEN WLEDIG was emperor of Rome, and he was a comelier man, and a better and a wiser. than any emperor that had been before him.[1] And one day he held a council of Kings, and he said to his friends, "I desire to go to-morrow to hunt." And the next day in the morning he set forth with his retinue, and came to the valley of the river that flowed towards Rome. And he hunted through the valley until midday. And with him also were two and thirty crowned kings, that were his vassals; not for the

[1] Maxen Wledig was an emperor at Rome. And the comeliest man was he, and the wisest, and the one that was most fit to be an emperor, of all that had been before him.

64

delight of hunting went the emperor with them, but to put himself on equal terms with those kings.[1]

And the sun was high in the sky over their heads, and the heat was great.   And sleep came upon Maxen Wledig.   And his attendants stood and set up their shields around him upon the shafts of their spears to protect him from the sun, and they placed a gold enamelled shield under his head, and so Maxen slept.

And he saw a dream.   And this is the dream that he saw.   He was journeying along the valley of the river towards its source; and he came to the highest mountain in the world.   And he thought that the mountain was as high as the sky; and when he came over the mountain, it seemed to him that he went through the fairest and most level regions that man ever yet beheld, on the other side of the mountain. And he saw large and mighty rivers descending from the mountain to the sea, and towards the mouths of the rivers he proceeded.   And as he journeyed thus, he came to the mouth of the largest river ever seen. And he beheld a great city at the entrance of the river, and a vast castle in the city, and he saw many high towers of various colours in the castle.   And he saw a fleet at the mouth of the river, the largest ever seen.   And he saw one ship among the fleet; larger was it by far, and fairer than all the others.   Of such part of the ship as he could see above the water, one plank was gilded and the other silvered over.   He saw a bridge of the bone of the whale from the ship to the land, and he thought that he went along the bridge and came into the ship.   And a sail was hoisted on the ship, and along the sea and the ocean was it borne.   Then it seemed that he came to the fairest

---

[1] Not for the delight of hunting went the emperor so far as that, but to make himself such a man that he would be lord over those kings.

island in the whole world, and he traversed the island
from sea to sea, even to the farthest shore of the
island. Valleys he saw, and steeps, and rocks of
wondrous height, and rugged precipices.[1] Never yet
saw he the like. And thence he beheld an island in the
sea, facing this rugged [2] land. And between him and
this island was a country of which the plain was as
large as the sea, the mountain as vast as the wood.

And from the mountain he saw a river that flowed
through the land and fell into the sea. And at the
mouth of the river, he beheld a castle, the fairest that
man ever saw, and the gate of the castle was open, and
he went into the castle. And in the castle he saw a
fair hall of which the roof seemed to be all gold, the
walls of the hall seemed to be entirely of glittering
precious gems, the doors all seemed to be of gold.
Golden seats he saw in the hall, and silver tables.
And on a seat opposite to him, he beheld two auburn-
haired youths playing at chess. He saw a silver board

[1] Valleys he saw, and precipices, and wondrous high rocks, and
a rugged, waterless land.
[2] Barren.

for the chess, and golden pieces thereon. The garments of the youths were of jet black satin, and chaplets of ruddy gold bound their hair, whereon were sparkling jewels of great price,[1] rubies, and gems, alternately with imperial stones. Buskins of new cordovan leather on their feet, fastened by slides of red gold.

And beside a pillar in the hall he saw a hoary-headed man, in a chair of ivory, with the figures of two eagles of ruddy gold thereon. Bracelets of gold were upon his arms, and many rings upon his hands, and a golden torquis about his neck; and his hair was bound with a golden diadem. He was of powerful aspect. A chessboard of gold was before him, and a rod of gold, and a steel file in his hand. And he was carving out chessmen.

And he saw a maiden sitting before him in a chair of ruddy gold. Not more easy than to gaze upon the sun when brightest, was it to look upon her by reason of her beauty. A vest of white silk was upon the maiden, with clasps of red gold at the breast; and a surcoat of gold tissue was upon her, and a frontlet of red gold upon her head, and rubies and gems were in the frontlet, alternating with pearls and imperial stones. And a girdle of ruddy gold was around her. She was the fairest sight that man ever beheld.

The maiden arose from her chair before him, and he threw his arms about the neck of the maiden, and they two sat down together in the chair of gold: and the chair was not less roomy for them both, than for the maiden alone. And as he had his arms about the maiden's neck, and his cheek by her cheek, behold, through the chafing of the dogs at their leashing, and the clashing of the shields as they struck against each

---

[1] Sparkling jewels laboriously wrought.

other, and the beating together of the shafts of the
spears, and the neighing of the horses and their prancing, the emperor awoke.

And when he awoke, nor spirit nor existence was
left him, because of the maiden whom he had seen in
his sleep, for the love of the maiden pervaded his
whole frame.[1]   Then his household spake unto him.
"Lord," said they "is it not past the time for thee to
take thy food?"   Thereupon the emperor mounted
his palfrey, the saddest man that mortal ever saw, and
went forth towards Rome.

And thus he was during the space of a week.
When they of the household went to drink wine and
mead out of golden vessels, he went not with any of
them.   When they went to listen to songs and tales,
he went not with them there; neither could he be
persuaded to do anything but sleep.   And as often as
he slept, he beheld in his dreams the maiden he loved
best; but except when he slept he saw nothing of her,
for he knew not where in the world she was.

One day the page of the chamber spake unto him;
now, although he was page of the chamber, he was
king of the Romans.   "Lord," said he, "all thy
people revile thee"   "Wherefore do they revile me?"
asked the emperor.   "Because they can get neither
message nor answer from thee, as men should have
from their lord.   This is the cause why thou art
spoken evil of."   "Youth," said the emperor, "do
thou bring unto me the wise men of Rome, and I
will tell them wherefore I am sorrowful."

Then the wise men of Rome were brought to the
emperor, and he spake to them.   "Sages of Rome,"
said he, "I have seen a dream.   And in the dream I

[1] There was no joint of his bones, or cavity of his nails, not to
speak of anything larger than these, that was not full of the
maiden's love.

beheld a maiden, and because of the maiden is there
neither life, nor spirit, nor existence within me."
"Lord," they answered, "since thou judgest us
worthy to counsel thee, we will give thee counsel.
And this is our counsel; that thou send messengers for
three years to the three parts of the world, to seek
for thy dream. And as thou knowest not what
day or what night good news may come to thee, the
hope thereof will support thee."

So the messengers journeyed for the space of a year
wandering about the world, and seeking tidings concerning his dream. But when they came back at the
end of the year they knew not one word more than
they did the day they set forth. And then was the
emperor exceeding sorrowful, for he thought that he
should never have tidings of her whom best he
loved.

Then spoke the king of the Romans unto the
emperor. "Lord," said he, "go forth to hunt by the
way that thou didst seem to go, whither it were to the
east or to the west." So the emperor went forth to
hunt, and he came to the bank of the river. "Behold,"
said he, "this is where I was when I saw the dream,
and I went towards the source of the river westward."

And thereupon thirteen messengers of the emperor's set forth, and before them they saw a high
mountain, which seemed to them to touch the sky.
Now this was the guise in which the messengers
journeyed; one sleeve was on the cap of each of
them in front; as a sign that they were messengers, in
order that through what hostile land soever they
might pass no harm might be done them. And when
they were come over this mountain they beheld vast
plains, and large rivers flowing therethrough.
"Behold," said they, "the land which our master
saw."

And they went along the mouths of the rivers, until they came to the mighty river which they saw flowing to the sea, and the vast city, and the many-coloured high towers in the castle. They saw the largest fleet in the world, in the harbour of the river, and one ship that was larger than any of the others. "Behold again," said they, "the dream that our master saw." And in·the great ship they crossed the sea, and came to the Island of Britain. And they traversed the island until they came to Snowdon. "Behold," said they, "the rugged [1] land that our master saw." And they went forward until they saw Anglesey before them, and until they saw Arvon likewise. "Behold," said they, "the land our master saw in his sleep." And they saw Aber Sain, and a castle at the mouth of the river. The portal of the castle saw they open, and into the castle they went, and they saw a hall in the castle. Then said they, "Behold the hall which he saw in his sleep."

They went into the hall, and they beheld two youths playing at chess on the golden bench. And they beheld the hoary-headed man beside the pillar, in the ivory chair, carving chessmen. And they beheld the maiden sitting on a chair of ruddy gold.

The messengers bent down upon their knees. "Empress of Rome, all hail!" "Ha, gentles," said the maiden, "ye bear the seeming of honourable men, and the badge of envoys, what mockery is this ye do to me?" "We mock thee not, lady, but the emperor of Rome hath seen thee in his sleep, and he has neither life nor spirit left because of thee. Thou shalt have of us therefore the choice, lady, whether thou wilt go with us and be made empress of Rome, or that the emperor come hither and take thee for his wife?" "Ha, lords," said the maiden, "I will not deny what

[1] Waterless.

you say, neither will I believe it too well. If the
emperor love me, let him come here to seek me."

And by day and night the messengers hied them
back. And when their horses failed, they bought
other fresh ones. And when they came to Rome they
saluted the emperor, and asked their boon, which was
given to them according as they named it. "We
will be thy guides, lord," said they, "over sea and over
land, to the place where is the woman whom best thou
lovest, for we know her name, and her kindred, and
her race."

And immediately the emperor set forth with his
army. And these men were his guides. Towards
the Island of Britain they went over the sea and the
deep. And he conquered the Island from Beli the
son of Manogan, and his sons, and drove them to the
sea, and went forward even unto Arvon. And the

emperor knew the land when he saw it. And when he beheld the castle of Aber Sain, " Look yonder," said he, " there is the castle wherein I saw the damsel whom I best love." And he went forward into the castle and into the hall, and there he saw Kynan the son of Eudav, and Adeon the son of Eudav, playing at chess. And he saw Eudav the son of Caradawc, sitting on a chair of ivory carving chessmen. And the maiden whom he had beheld in his sleep, he saw sitting on a chair of gold. " Empress of Rome," said he, "all hail!" And the emperor threw his arms about her neck ; and that night she became his bride.

And the next day in the morning, the damsel asked her maiden portion. And he told her to name what she would, and she asked to have the Island of Britain for her father, from the Channel to the Irish Sea, together with the three adjacent islands to hold under the empress of Rome ; and to have three chief castles made for her, in whatever places she might choose in the Island of Britain. And she chose to have the highest castle made at Arvon. And they brought thither earth from Rome that it mght be more healthful for the emperor to sleep, and sit, and walk upon. After that the two other castles were made for her, which were Caerlleon and Caermarthen.

And one day, the emperor went to hunt at Caermarthen, and he came so far as the top of Brevi Vawr, and there the emperor pitched his tent. And that encamping place is called Cadeir Maxen, even to this day. And because that he built the castle with a myriad of men, he called it Caervyrddin. Then Helen bethought her to make high roads from one castle to another throughout the Island of Britain. And the roads were made. And for this cause are they called the roads of Helen Luyddawc,[1] that she

[1] Helen of the Legions.

was sprung from a native of this island, and the men of the Island of Britain would not have made these great roads [1] for any save for her.

Seven years did the emperor tarry in this Island. Now, at that time, the men of Rome had a custom that whatsoever emperor should remain in other lands more than seven years, should remain to his own overthrow, and should never return to Rome again.

So they made a new emperor. And this one wrote a letter of threat to Maxen. There was nought in the letter but only this, "If thou comest, and if thou ever comest to Rome." And even unto Caerlleon came this letter to Maxen, and these tidings. Then sent he a letter to the man who styled himself emperor in Rome. There was nought in that letter also but only this, "If I come to Rome, and if I come."

And thereupon Maxen set forth towards Rome with his army, and vanquished France and Burgundy, and every land on the way, and sat down before the city of Rome.

A year was the emperor before the city, and he was no nearer taking it than the first day. And after him there came the brothers of Helen Luyddawc from the Island of Britain, and a small host with them, and better warriors were in that small host than twice as many Romans. And the emperor was told that a host was seen, halting close to his army and encamping, and no man ever saw a fairer or better appointed host for its size, nor more handsome standards.

And Helen went to see the hosts, and she knew the standards of her brothers. Then came Kynan the son of Eudav, and Adeon the son of Eudav, to meet the emperor. And the emperor was glad because of them, and embraced them.

[1] Legions.

Then they looked at the Romans as they attacked
the city. Said Kynan to his brother, "We will try
to attack the city more expertly than this." So they
measured by night the height of the wall, and they
sent their carpenters to the wood, and a ladder was
made for every four men of their number. Now
when these were ready, every day at mid-day the
emperors went to meat, and they ceased to fight on
both sides till all had finished eating. And in the
morning the men of Britain took their food, and they
drank until they were invigorated. And while the two
emperors were at meat, the Britons came to the city,[1]
and placed their ladders against it, and forthwith they
came in through the city.

The new emperor had not time to arm himself
when they fell upon him, and slew him and many
others with him. And three nights and three days
were they subduing the men that were in the city
and taking the castle. And others of them kept the
city, lest any of the host of Maxen should come
therein, until they had subjected all to their will.

Then spake Maxen to Helen Luyddawc, "I marvel,
lady," said he, "that thy brothers have not conquered
this city for me,"[2] "Lord, emperor," she answered,
"the wisest youths in the world are my brothers. Go
thou thither and ask the city of them, and if it be in
their possession thou shalt have it gladly." So the
emperor and Helen went and demanded the city And
they told the emperor that none had taken the city,
and that none could give it him, but the men of the
Island of Britain. Then the gates of the city of
Rome were opened, and the emperor sat on the
throne and all the men of Rome submitted themselves unto him.

[1] Over the wall into the city.
[2] That it was not for me that thy brothers conquered the city.

The emperor then said unto Kynan and Adeon,
"Lords," said he, "I have now had possession of the
whole of my empire. This host give I unto you to
vanquish whatever region ye may desire in the
world."

So they set forth and conquered lands, and castles
and cities. And they slew all the men, but the
women they kept alive. And thus they continued
until the young men that had come with them were
grown grey-headed, from the length of time they were
upon this conquest.

Then spoke Kynan unto Adeon his brother,.
"Whether wilt thou rather," said he, "tarry in this
land, or go back into the land whence thou didst
come forth?"   Now he chose to go back to his own
land and many with him. But Kynan tarried there
with the other part, and dwelt there.

.And they took counsel and cut out the tongues of the women, lest they should corrupt their speech. And because of the silence of the women from their own speech, the men of Armorica are called Britons. From that time there came frequently, and still comes, that language from the Island of Britain.

And this tale is called the Dream of Maxen Wledig, emperor of Rome. And here it ends.

THE LADY OF THE FOUNTAIN.

KING ARTHUR[1] was at Caerlleon upon Usk; and
one day he sat in his chamber; and with him
were Owain the son of Urien, and Kynon the
son of Clydno, and Kai the son of Kyner; and
Gwenhwyvar and her hand-maidens at needlework
by the window. And if it should be said that
there was a porter at Arthur's palace, there was
none. Glewlwyd Gavaelvawr was there, acting as
porter, to welcome guests and strangers, and to
receive them with honour, and to inform them of

[1] "The Emperor Arthur" all through the tale.

the manners and customs of the Court; and to direct those who came to the Hall or to the presence chamber, and those who came to take up their lodging.[1]

In the centre of the chamber king Arthur sat, upon a seat of green rushes, over which was spread a covering of flame-coloured satin; and a cushion of red satin was under his elbow.

Then Arthur spoke, "If I thought you would not disparage me," said he, "I would sleep while I wait for my repast; and you can entertain one another with relating tales, and can obtain a flagon of mead and some meat from Kai." And the King went to sleep. And Kynon the son of Clydno asked Kai for that which Arthur had promised them. "I too will have the good tale which he promised to me," said Kai. "Nay," answered Kynon, "fairer will it be for thee to fulfil Arthur's behest in the first place, and then we will tell thee the best tale that we know." So Kai went to the kitchen and to the mead-cellar, and returned, bearing a flagon of mead, and a golden goblet, and a handful of skewers upon which were broiled collops of meat. Then they ate the collops and began to drink the mead. "Now" said Kai, "it is time for you to give me my story." "Kynon," said Owain, "do thou pay to Kai the tale that is his due." "Truly," said Kynon, "thou art older, and are a better teller of tales, and hast seen more marvellous things than I; do thou therefore pay Kai his tale." "Begin

[1] To begin to honour them, to inform them of the manners and the customs of the Court, those he was told were to go to the hall or the presence chamber, and those he was told were to get lodging.

thyself," quoth Owain, "with the best that thou knowest." "I will do so," answered Kynon.

"I was the only son of my mother and father; and I was exceedingly aspiring, and my daring was very great. I thought there was no enterprise' in the world too mighty for me, and after I had achieved all the adventures that were in my own country,[1] I equipped myself, and set forth to journey through deserts, and distant regions. And at length it chanced that I came to the fairest valley in the world, wherein were trees of equal growth; and a river ran through the valley, and a path was by the side of the river. And I followed the path until mid-day, and continued my journey along the remainder of the valley until the evening; and at the extremity of a plain I came to a large and lustrous Castle, at the foot of which was a torrent. And I approached the Castle, and there I beheld two youths, with yellow curling hair, each with a frontlet of gold upon his head, and clad in a garment of yellow satin; and they had gold clasps upon their insteps. In the hand of each of them was an ivory bow, strung with the sinews of the stag; and their arrows had their shafts of the bone of the whale, and were winged with peacock's feathers. The shafts also had golden heads. And they had daggers with blades of gold, and with hilts of the bone of the whale. And they were shooting their daggers.

"And a little way from them, I saw a man[2] in the prime of life, with his beard newly shorn, clad in a robe and a mantle of yellow satin; and round the

---

[1] And I did not think there was in the world a wrong too mighty for me to set right. And when I had set right all the wrongs that were in my own country.

[2] Add " with fair curly hair."

top of his mantle was a band of gold lace. On his feet were shoes of variegated leather, fastened by two bosses of gold. When I saw him, I went towards him and saluted him; and such was his courtesy, that he no sooner received my greeting than he returned it.[1] And he went with me towards the Castle. Now there were no dwellers in the Castle, except those who were in one hall. And there I saw four and twenty damsels, embroidering satin, at a window. And this I tell thee, Kai, that[2] the least fair of them was fairer than the fairest maid thou didst ever behold, in the Island of Britain; and the least lovely of them was more lovely than Gwenhwyvar, the wife of Arthur, when she appeared loveliest at the Offering, on the day of the Nativity, or at the feast of Easter.[3] They rose up at my coming, and six of them took my horse, and divested me of my armour; and six others took my arms, and washed them in a vessel, until they were perfectly bright. And the third six spread cloths upon the tables, and prepared meat. And the fourth six took off my soiled garments, and placed others upon me; namely, an under vest and a doublet of fine linen, and a robe, and a surcoat, and a mantle of yellow satin, and a broad gold band upon the mantle. And they placed cushions both beneath and around me, with coverings of red linen. And I sat down. Now the six maidens who had taken my horse, unharnessed him, as well as if they had been the best Squires in the Island of Britain. Then, behold, they

---

[1] And such was his courtesy that he greeted me before I could greet him.

[2] Add, "I ween that."

[3] When she was ever loveliest, at Christmas, or at Easter-tide mass.

brought bowls of silver wherein was water to wash ;
and towels of linen, some green and some white ; and
I washed. And in a little while the man sat down
to the table.[1] And I sat next to him, and below me
sat all the maidens, except those who waited on us.
And the table was of silver ; and the cloths upon
the table were of linen. And no vessel was served
upon the table that was not either of gold, or of
silver, or of buffalo horn. And our meat was
brought to us. And verily, Kai, I saw there every
sort of meat, and every sort of liquor, that I ever
saw elsewhere ; but the meat and the liquors were
better served there, than I ever saw them in any
other place.

"Until the repast was half over, neither the man
nor any one of the damsels spoke a single word to
me ; but when the man perceived that it would be
more agreeable to me to converse than to eat any
more, he began to enquire of me who I was. I said
I was glad to find that there was some one who
would discourse with me, and that it was not considered so great a crime at that Court, for people
to hold converse together. 'Chieftain,' said the man,
'we would have talked to thee sooner, but we feared
to disturb thee during thy repast. Now, however,
we will discourse.' Then I told the man who I
was, and what was the cause of my journey. And
said that I was seeking whether any one was superior.
to me, or whether I could gain the mastery over all.
The man looked upon me, and he smiled, and said,
'If I did not fear to distress thee too much,[2] I would
shew thee that which thou seekest.' Upon this I
became anxious and sorrowful ; and when the man

[1] And the man I had seen erstwhile sat down to the table.
[2] Did I not think that too much trouble would befall thee.

perceived it, he said, 'If thou wouldst rather that
I should shew thee thy disadvantage, than thine
advantage, I will do so. Sleep here to-night, and
in the morning, arise early, and take the road upwards through the valley, until thou reachest the
wood, through which thou camest hither. A little
way within the wood, thou wilt meet with a road,
branching off to the right; by which thou must
proceed, until thou comest to a large sheltered glade,
with a mound in the centre. And thou wilt see
a black man of great stature, on the top of the
mound; he is not smaller in size than two of the
men of this world. He has but one foot, and one
eye, in the middle of his forehead. And he has a
club of iron, and it is certain that there are no two
men in the world, who would not find their burden
in that club. And he is not a comely man, but
on the contrary he is exceedingly ill favoured; and
he is the woodward of that wood. And thou wilt
see a thousand wild animals, grazing around him.
Enquire of him the way out of the glade, and he
will reply to thee briefly,[1] and will point out the
road, by which thou shalt find that which thou art
in quest of.'

"And long seemed the night to me. And the
next morning I arose, and equipped myself, and
mounted my horse, and proceeded straight through
the valley, to the wood, and I followed the cross-
road which the man had pointed out to me, till at
length I arrived at the glade. And there was I
three times more astonished at the number of wild
animals that I beheld, than the man had said I
should be. And the black man was there, sitting
upon the top of the mound. Huge of stature as the

----

[1] With querulous roughness.

man had told me that he was, I found him to exceed
by far the description he had given me of him. As
for the iron club, which the man had told me was
a burden for two men, I am certain, Kai, that it would
be a heavy weight for four warriors to lift. And this
was in the black man's hand. And he only spoke to
me in answer to my questions.[1] Then I asked him
what power he held over those animals. 'I will shew
thee, little man,' said he. And he took his club in
his hand, and with it he struck a stag a great blow,
so that he brayed vehemently, and at his braying, the
animals came together, as numerous as the stars in
the sky, so that it was difficult for me to find room
in the glade, to stand among them. There were
serpents, and dragons, and divers sorts of animals.
And he looked at them, and bade them go and
feed. And they bowed their heads, and did him
homage, as vassals to their lord.

"Then the black man said to me, 'Seest thou now,
little man, what power I hold over these animals?'
Then I enquired of him the way; and he became
very rough in his manner to me; however he asked
me whither I would go. And when I had told him
who I was, and what I sought, he directed me.
'Take,' said he, 'that path that leads towards the
head of the glade, and ascend the wooded steep,
until thou comest to its summit; and there thou
wilt find an open space, like to a large valley, and in
the midst of it a tall tree, whose branches are greener
than the greenest pine trees. Under this tree is a
fountain, and by the side of the fountain, a marble slab,
and on the marble slab a silver bowl, attached by a
chain of silver, so that it may not be carried away.[2]

[1] And he would but bandy words with me.
[2] So that they cannot be separated.

Take the bowl, and throw a bowlful of water upon
the slab, and thou wilt hear a mighty peal of thunder ;
so that thou wilt think that heaven and earth are
trembling with its fury. With the thunder there will
come a shower so severe, that it will be scarcely
possible for thee to endure it and live. And the
shower will be of hailstones. And after the shower,
the weather will become fair ; but every leaf that was
upon the tree will have been carried away by the
shower. Then a flight of birds will come and alight
upon the tree ; and in thine own country thou didst
never hear a strain so sweet, as that which they will
sing. And at the moment thou art most delighted
with the song of the birds, thou wilt hear a murmuring and complaining coming towards thee along the
valley. And thou wilt see a knight upon a coal black
horse, clothed in black velvet, and with a pennon of
black linen upon his lance, and he will ride unto
thee to encounter thee, with the utmost speed. If
thou fleest from him he will overtake thee, and if
thou abidest there, as sure as thou art a mounted
knight, he will leave thee on foot. And if thou dost
not find trouble in that adventure, thou needst not
seek it during the rest of thy life.'

"So I journeyed on, until I reached the summit
of the steep. And there I found every thing, as
the black man had described it to me. And I went
up to the tree, and beneath it I saw the fountain,
and by its side the marble slab ; and the silver bowl,
fastened by the chain. Then I took the bowl, and
cast a bowlful of water upon the slab ; and thereupon
behold the thunder came, much more violent than
the black man had led me to expect ; and after the
thunder came the shower ; and of a truth I tell thee,
Kai, that there is neither man nor beast that could

endure that shower and live. For not one of those hailstones would be stopped either by the flesh, or by the skin, until it had reached the bone. I turned my horse's flanks towards the shower, and placed the beak of my shield over his head and neck, while I held the upper part of it over my own head. And thus I withstood the shower. When I looked on the tree, there was not a single leaf upon it, and then the sky became clear ; and with that, behold the birds lighted upon the tree, and sang. And truly, Kai, I never heard any melody equal to that, either before or since. And when I was most charmed with listening to the birds, lo, a murmuring voice was heard through the valley, approaching me, and saying, ' Oh, Knight, what has brought thee hither? What evil have I done to thee, that thou shouldest act towards me and my possessions, as thou hast this day? Dost thou not know that the shower to-day has left in my dominions neither man nor beast alive, that was exposed to it?' And thereupon, behold a Knight on a black horse appeared, clothed in jet black velvet, and with a tabard of black linen about him. And we charged each other ; and as the onset was furious, it was not long before I was overthrown. Then the Knight passed the shaft of his lance through the bridle rein of my horse, and rode off with the two horses ; leaving me where I was. And he did not even bestow so much notice upon me, as to imprison me, nor did he despoil me of my arms. So I returned along the road by which I had come. And when I reached the glade where the black man was, I confess to thee, Kai, it is a marvel that I did not melt down into a liquid pool, through the shame that I felt at the black man's derision. And that night I came to the same Castle, where I had spent the night pre-

ceding. And I was more agreeably entertained that
night, than I had been the night before; and I was
better feasted, and I conversed freely with the inmates
of the Castle; and none of them alluded to my expedition to the fountain, neither did I mention it to
any. And I remained there that night. When I
arose on the morrow, I found ready saddled a dark-
bay palfrey, with nostrils as red as scarlet. And after
putting on my armour, and leaving there my blessing,
I returned to my own Court. And that horse I still
possess, and he is in the stable yonder. And I
declare that I would not part with him for the best
palfrey in the Island of Britain.

"Now of a truth, Kai, no man ever before con-
fessed to an adventure so much to his own discredit;
and verily it seems strange to me, that neither before
nor since have I heard of any person, besides myself,
who knew of this adventure, and that the subject of
it should exist within King Arthur's dominions, without any other person lighting upon it."

"Now," quoth Owain, "would it not be well to go
and endeavour to discover that place?"

"By the hand of my friend," said Kai, "often dost
thou utter that with thy tongue, which thou wouldest
not make good with thy deeds."

"In very truth," said Gwenhwyvar, "it were better
thou wert hanged, Kai, than to use such uncourteous
speech towards a man like Owain."

"By the hand of my friend, good Lady," said
Kai, "thy praise of Owain is not greater than
mine."

With that Arthur awoke, and asked if he had not
been sleeping a little.

"Yes, Lord," answered Owain, "thou hast slept
awhile."

"Is it time for us to go to meat?"

"It is, Lord," said Owain.

Then the horn .for washing was sounded, and the King and all his household sat down to eat. And when the meal was ended, Owain withdrew to his lodging, and made ready his horse and his arms.

On the morrow, with the dawn of day, he put on his armour, and mounted his charger, and travelled through distant lands, and over desert mountains. And at length he arrived at the valley which Kynon had described to him; and he was certain that it was the same that he sought. And journeying along the valley, by the side of the river, he followed its course till he came to the plain, and within sight of the Castle. When he approached the Castle, he saw the youths shooting their daggers, in the place where Kynon had seen them; and the yellow man, to whom the Castle belonged, standing hard by. And no sooner had Owain saluted the yellow man, than he was saluted by him in return.

And he went forward towards the Castle, and there he saw the chamber; and when he had entered the chamber, he beheld the maidens working at satin embroidery, in chairs of gold. And their beauty, and their comeliness seemed to Owain far greater than Kynon had represented to him. And they arose to wait upon Owain, as they had done to Kynon. And the meal which they set before him, gave more satisfaction to Owain than it had done to Kynon.

About the middle of the repast the yellow man asked Owain the object of his journey. And Owain made it known to him, and said, "I am in quest of the Knight who guards the fountain." Upon this, the yellow man smiled, and said that he was as loth to point out that adventure to Owain as he had been to Kynon. However he described the whole to Owain, and they retired to rest.

The next morning Owain found his horse made ready for him by the damsels, and he set forward and came to the glade where the black man was. And the stature of the black man seemed more wonderful to Owain, than it had done to Kynon, and Owain asked of him his road, and he showed it to him. And Owain followed the road, as Kynon had done, till he came to the green tree; and he beheld the fountain, and the slab beside the fountain with the bowl upon it. And Owain took the bowl, and threw a bowlful of water upon the slab. And lo, the thunder was heard, and after the thunder came the shower, much more violent than Kynon had described, and after the shower, the sky became bright. And when Owain looked at the tree, there was not one leaf upon it. And immediately the birds came, and settled upon the tree, and sang. And when their song was most pleasing to Owain, he beheld a Knight coming towards him through the valley, and he prepared to receive him; and encountered him violently. Having broken both their lances, they drew their swords, and fought blade to blade. Then Owain struck the Knight a blow through his helmet, head piece and visor, and through the skin, and the flesh, and the bone, until it wounded the very brain. Then the black Knight felt that he had received a mortal wound, upon which he turned his horse's head, and fled. And Owain pursued him, and followed close upon him, although he was not near enough to strike him with his sword. Thereupon Owain descried a vast and resplendent Castle. And they came to the Castle gate. And the black Knight was allowed to enter, and the portcullis was let fall

upon Owain ; and it struck his horse behind the
saddle, and cut him in two, and carried away the
rowels of the spurs that were upon Owain's heels.
And the portcullis descended to the floor. And
the rowels of the spurs and part of the horse were
without, and Owain, with the other part of the horse
remained between the two gates, and the inner gate
was closed, so that Owain could not go thence ; and
Owain was in a perplexing situation. And while he
was in this state, he could see through an aperture in
the gate, a street facing him, with a row of houses on
each side. And he beheld a maiden, with yellow
curling hair, and a frontlet of gold upon her head ;
and she was clad in a dress of yellow satin, and on
her feet were shoes of variegated leather. And she
approached the gate, and desired that it should be
opened. "Heaven knows, Lady," said Owain, "it
is no more possible for me to open to thee from
hence, than it is for thee to set me free." "Truly,"
said the damsel, "it is very sad that thou canst not
be released, and every woman ought to succour thee,
for I never saw one more faithful in the service of
ladies than thou. As a friend thou art the most
sincere, and as a lover the most devoted. Therefore," quoth she, "whatever is in my power to do
for thy release, I will do it. Take this ring and put
it on thy finger, with the stone inside thy hand ;
and close thy hand upon the stone. And as long
as thou concealest it, it will conceal thee. When
they have consulted together, they will come forth
to fetch thee, in order to put thee to death ;[1] and
they will be much grieved that they cannot find thee.
And I will await thee on the horseblock yonder ; and
thou wilt be able to see me, though I cannot see thee ;

[1] Add "On account of the knight."

therefore come and place thy hand upon my shoulder, that I may know that thou art near me. And by the way that I go hence, do thou accompany me. Then she went away from Owain, and he did all that the maiden had told him. And the people of the Castle came to seek Owain, to put him to death, and when they found nothing but the half of his horse, they were sorely grieved.

And Owain vanished from among them, and went to the maiden, and placed his hand upon her shoulder, whereupon she set off, and Owain followed her, until they came to the door of a large and beautiful chamber, and the maiden opened it, and they went in, and closed the door. And Owain looked around the chamber, and behold there was not even a single nail in it, that was not painted with gorgeous colours; and there was not a single panel, that had not sundry images [1] in gold portrayed upon it.

The maiden kindled a fire, and took water in a silver bowl, and put a towel of white linen on her shoulder, and gave Owain water to wash. Then she placed before him a silver table, inlaid with gold; upon which was a cloth of yellow linen; and she brought him food. And of a truth, Owain never saw any kind of meat that was not there in abundance, but it was better cooked there, than he ever found it in any other place. Nor did he ever see so excellent a display of meat and drink as there. And there was not one vessel from which he was served, that was not of gold, or of silver. And Owain ate and drank, until late in the afternoon, when lo, they heard a mighty clamour in the Castle; and Owain asked the maiden what that outcry was. "They are administering extreme unction," said she, "to the

_____
[1] An image of a different kind.

Nobleman who owns the Castle." And Owain went to sleep.

The couch which the maiden had prepared for him was meet for Arthur himself; it was of scarlet, and fur, and satin, and sendall, and fine linen. In the middle of the night they heard a woeful outcry. "What outcry again is this?" said Owain. "The Nobleman who owned the Castle is now dead," said the maiden. And a little after daybreak, they heard an exceeding loud clamour and wailing. And Owain asked the maiden what was the cause of it. "They are bearing to the church, the body of the Nobleman who owned the Castle."

And Owain rose up, and clothed himself, and opened a window of the chamber, and looked towards the Castle; and he could see neither the bounds, nor the extent of the hosts that filled the streets. And they were fully armed; and a vast number of women were with them, both on horseback, and on foot; and all the ecclesiastics in the city, singing. And it seemed to Owain that the sky resounded with the vehemence of their cries, and with the noise of the trumpets, and with the singing of the ecclesiastics.[1] In the midst of the throng, he beheld the bier, over which was a veil of white linen; and wax tapers were burning beside, and around it, and none that supported the bier was lower in rank than a powerful[2] Baron.

Never did Owain see an assemblage so gorgeous with satin, and silk, and sendall. And following the train, he beheld a lady with yellow hair falling over her shoulders, and stained with blood; and about her a dress of yellow satin, which was torn. Upon her feet were shoes of variegated leather. And it was a

---

[1] Monks.   [2] Land-owning.

marvel that the ends of her fingers were not bruised, from the violence with which she smote her hands together. Truly she would have been the fairest lady Owain ever saw, had she been in her usual guise. And her cry was louder than the shout of the men, or the clamour of the trumpets.[1] No sooner had he beheld the lady, than he became inflamed with her love, so that it took entire possession of him.

Then he enquired of the maiden who the lady was. " Heaven knows," replied the maiden, " she may be said to be the fairest, and the most chaste, and the most liberal, and the wisest, and the most noble of women. And she is my mistress; and she is called the Countess of the Fountain, the wife of him whom thou didst slay yesterday." " Verily," said Owain "she is the woman that I love best." " Verily," said the maiden, "she shall also love thee not a little."

And with that the maid arose, and kindled a fire, and filled a pot with water, and placed it to warm; and she brought a towel of white linen, and placed it around Owain's neck; and she took a goblet of ivory, and a silver basin, and filled them with warm water, wherewith she washed Owain's head. Then she opened a wooden casket, and drew forth a razor, whose haft was of ivory, and upon which were two rivets of gold. And she shaved his beard, and she dried his head, and his throat, with the towel. Then she rose up from before Owain, and brought him to eat. And truly Owain had never so good a meal, nor was he ever so well served.

When he had finished his repast, the maiden arranged his couch. "Come here," said she, "and

[1] Louder was her cry than any trumpet blast that arose from among the multitude.

sleep, and I will go and woo for thee." And Owain
went to sleep, and the maiden shut the door of the
chamber after her, and went towards the Castle
When she came there, she found nothing but mourn-
ing, and sorrow; and the Countess in her chamber
could not bear the sight of any one through grief.
Luned came and saluted her, but the Countess
answered her not. And the maiden bent down
towards her, and said, "What aileth thee, that thou
answerest no one to-day?" "Luned," said the
Countess, "what change hath befallen thee, that
thou hast not come to visit me in my grief? It was
wrong in thee, and I having made thee rich; it was
wrong in thee that thou didst not come to see me in
my distress. That was wrong in thee." "Truly,"
said Luned, "I thought thy good sense was greater
than I find it to be. Is it well for thee to mourn
after that good man, or for anything else, that thou
canst not have?" "I declare to heaven," said the
Countess, "that in the whole world there is not a
man equal to him." "Not so," said Luned, "for an
ugly man would be as good as, or better than he." [1]
"I declare to heaven," said the Countess, "that were
it not repugnant to me to cause to be put to death
one whom I have brought up, I would have thee
executed, for making such a comparison to me.
As it is, I will banish thee." "I am glad," said
Luned, "that thou hast no other cause to do so,
than that I would have been of service to thee when

[1] "Truly," said Luned, "I thought thy good sense was greater
than I find it to be. Is it better to grieve because thou canst not
get *that* good man, than it is to grieve for anything else thou
canst never get?" "I declare to heaven," said the Countess,
"that I could never get my lord in any other man, be he the
best in the world." "Oh yes," said Luned, "thou couldst
marry a husband that would be as good as he, or better than he."

thou didst not know what was to thine advantage.
And henceforth evil betide whichever of us shall make
the first advance towards reconciliation to the other;
whether I should seek an invitation from thee, or
thou of thine own accord shouldest seek to invite me."

With that Luned went forth; and the Countess
arose and followed her to the door of the chamber,
and began coughing loudly. And when Luned looked
back, the Countess beckoned to her; and she returned to the Countess. "In truth," said the
Countess, "evil is thy disposition; but if thou
knowest what is to my advantage, declare it to me."
"I will do so," quoth she.

"Thou knowest that except by warfare and arms
it is impossible for thee to preserve thy possessions;
delay not, therefore, to seek some one who can defend
them." "And how can I do that?" said the Countess.
"I will tell thee," said Luned, "unless thou canst
defend the fountain, thou canst not maintain thy
dominions; and no one can defend the fountain,
except it be a knight of Arthur's household; and I
will go to Arthur's court, and ill betide me, if I return
thence without a warrior who can guard the fountain,
as well as, or even better than, he who defended it
formerly." "That will be hard to perform," said the
Countess. "Go, however, and make proof of that
which thou hast promised."

Luned set out, under the pretence of going to
Arthur's court; but she went back to the chamber
where she had left Owain; and she tarried there
with him as long as it might have taken her to have
travelled to the Court of King Arthur. And at the
end of that time, she apparelled herself, and went to
visit the Countess. And the Countess was much
rejoiced when she saw her, and enquired what news

she brought from the Court.   " I bring thee the best
of news," said Luned, "for I have compassed the
object of my mission.   When wilt thou, that I should
present to thee the chieftain who has come with me
hither ? "   " Bring him here to visit me to-morrow,
at mid-day," said the Countess, "and I will cause the
town to be assembled by that time."

And Luned returned home.   And the next day, at
noon, Owain arrayed himself in a coat, and a surcoat,
and a mantle of yellow satin, upon which was a broad
band of gold lace; and on his feet were high shoes
of variegated leather, which were fastened by golden
clasps, in the form of lions.   And they proceeded to
the chamber of the Countess.

Right glad was the Countess of their coming.   And
she gazed steadfastly upon Owain, and said, " Luned,
this knight has not the look of a traveller."   "What
harm is there in that, Lady ? " said Luned.   " I am
certain," said the Countess, "that no other man than
this, chased the soul from the body of my lord."
" So much the better for thee, Lady," said Luned,
" for had he not been stronger than thy lord, he could
not have deprived him of life.   There is no remedy
for that which is past, be it as it may."   " Go back
to thine abode," said the Countess, "and I will take
counsel."

The next day, the Countess caused all her subjects
to assemble, and shewed them that her Earldom was
left defenceless, and that it could not be protected
but with horse and arms, and military skill.   " Therefore," said she, " this is what I offer for your choice :
either let one of you take me, or give your consent
for me to take a husband from elsewhere, to defend
my dominions."

So they came to the determination, that it was

C

better that she should have permission to marry
some one from elsewhere; and thereupon she sent
for the Bishops and Archbishops, to celebrate her
nuptials with Owain. And the men of the Earldom
did Owain homage.

And Owain defended the Fountain with lance and
sword. And this is the manner in which he defended
it. Whensoever a knight came there, he overthrew
him, and sold him for his full worth. And what he
thus gained, he divided among his Barons, and his
Knights; and no man in the whole world could be
more beloved than he was by his subjects. And it
was thus for the space of three years.

It befell that as Gwalchmai went forth one day
with King Arthur, he perceived him to be very sad
and sorrowful. And Gwalchmai was much grieved
to see Arthur in this state; and he questioned him,
saying, "Oh my Lord! what has befallen thee?"
"In sooth, Gwalchmai," said Arthur, "I am grieved
concerning Owain, whom I have lost these three
years; and I shall certainly die, if the fourth year
passes without my seeing him. Now I am sure, that
it is through the tale which Kynon the son of Clydno
related, that I have lost Owain." "There is no
need for thee," said Gwalchmai, "to summon to arms
thy whole dominions, on that account; for thou thyself, and the men of thy household, will be able to
avenge Owain, if he be slain; or to set him free, if
he be in prison; and if alive, to bring him back with
thee." And it was settled, according to what Gwalchmai had said.

Then Arthur and the men of his household prepared to go and seek Owain; and their number was
three thousand, beside their attendants. And Kynon

the son of Clydno acted as their guide. And Arthur
came to the Castle, where Kynon had been before.
And when he came there the youths were shooting
in the same place, and the yellow man was standing
hard by. When the yellow man saw Arthur, he
greeted him, and invited him to the Castle. And
Arthur accepted his invitation, and they entered the
Castle together. And great as was the number of
his retinue, their presence was scarcely observed in
the Castle, so vast was its extent. And the maidens
rose up to wait on them. And the service of the
maidens appeared to them all to excel any attendance
they had ever met with; and even the pages who
had charge of the horses, were no worse served, that
night, than Arthur himself would have been, in his
own Palace.

The next morning, Arthur set out thence, with
Kynon for his guide, and came to the place where
the black man was. And the stature of the black
man was more surprising to Arthur, than it had been
represented to him. And they came to the top of
the wooded steep, and traversed the valley, till they
reached the green tree; where they saw the fountain,
and the bowl and the slab. And upon that, Kai
came to Arthur, and spoke to him. "My Lord,"
said he, "I know the meaning of all this, and my
request is, that thou wilt permit me to throw the
water on the slab, and to receive the first advantage
that may befall." And Arthur gave him leave.

Then Kai threw a bowlful of water upon the slab,
and immediately there came the thunder, and after
the thunder the shower. And such a thunderstorm
they had never known before. And many of the
attendants who were in Arthur's train were killed by
the shower. After the shower had ceased, the sky

became clear. And on looking at the tree, they
beheld it completely leafless. Then the birds descended upon the tree. And the song of the birds
was far sweeter than any strain they had ever heard
before. Then they beheld a Knight, on a coal-black
horse, clothed in black satin, coming rapidly towards

them. And Kai met him and encountered him, and
it was not long before Kai was overthrown. And the
Knight withdrew.[1] And Arthur and his host encamped for the night.

And when they arose in the morning, they perceived the signal of combat upon the lance of the
Knight ; and Kai came to Arthur, and spoke to him.

[1] Encamped.

"My Lord," said he, "though I was overthrown yesterday, if it seem good to thee, I would gladly meet the Knight again to-day." "Thou mayst do so," said Arthur. And Kai went towards the Knight. And on the spot he overthrew Kai,[1] and struck him with the head of his lance in the forehead, so that it broke his helmet and the headpiece, and pierced the skin, and the flesh, the breadth of the spear-head, even to the bone. And Kai returned to his companions.

After this, all the household of Arthur went forth, one after the other, to combat the Knight, until there was not one that was not overthrown by him, except Arthur and Gwalchmai. And Arthur armed himself to encounter the Knight. "Oh, my lord," said Gwalchmai, "permit me to fight with him first." And Arthur permitted him. And he went forth to meet the Knight, having over himself and his horse, a satin robe of honour which had been sent him by the daughter of the Earl of Rhangyw, and in this dress he was not known by any of the host. And they charged each other, and fought all that day until the evening. And neither of them was able to un-horse the other.

The next day they fought with strong lances; and neither of them could obtain the mastery.

And the third day they fought with exceeding strong lances. And they were increased with rage, and fought furiously, even until noon. And they gave each other such a shock, that the girths of their horses were broken, so that they fell over their horses' cruppers to the ground. And they rose up speedily, and drew their swords, and resumed the combat.[2]

---

[1] Add "and looked at him."
[2] And belaboured each other.

And the multitude that witnessed the encounter felt
assured that they had never before seen two men so
valiant, or so powerful.   And had it been midnight,
it would have been light from the fire that flashed
from their weapons.   And the Knight gave Gwalchmai
a blow that turned his helmet from off his face, so
that the Knight knew that it was Gwalchmai.   Then
Owain said, " My lord Gwalchmai, I did not know
thee for my cousin, owing to the robe of honour,
that enveloped thee; take my sword and my arms."
Said Gwalchmai, " Thou, Owain, art the victor; take
thou my sword."   And with that Arthur saw that they
were conversing, and advanced towards them.   " My
lord Arthur," said Gwalchmai, "here is Owain, who
has vanquished me, and will not take my arms."
" My lord," said Owain, "it is he that has vanquished
me, and he will not take my sword."   " Give me your
swords," said Arthur, " and then neither of you has
vanquished the other."   Then Owain put his arms
around Arthur's neck, and they embraced.   And all
the host hurried forward to see Owain, and to em-
brace him.   And there was nigh being a loss of life,
so great was the press.

And they retired that night, and the next day Arthur
prepared to depart.   " My lord," said Owain, "this
is not well of thee.   For I have been absent from thee
these three years,[1] and during all that time, up to this
very day, I have been preparing a banquet for thee,
knowing that thou wouldest come to seek me.   Tarry
with me therefore, until thou and thy attendants have
recovered the fatigues of the journey, and have been
anointed."

And they all proceeded to the Castle of the Countess
of the Fountain, and the banquet which had been

[1] Add "and this is my abode."

three years preparing was consumed in three months.
Never had they a more delicious or agreeable banquet.
And Arthur prepared to depart. Then he sent an
embassy to the Countess, to beseech her to permit
Owain to go with him, for the space of three months,
that he might shew him to the nobles, and the fair
dames of the Island of Britain. And the Countess
gave her consent, although it was very painful to her.
So Owain came with Arthur to the Island of Britain.
And when he was once more amongst his kindred and
friends, he remained three years, instead of three
months, with them.

And as Owain one day sat at meat, in the City of
Caerlleon upon Usk, behold a damsel entered, upon
a bay horse, with a curling mane, and covered with
foam ; and the bridle, and as much as was seen of the
saddle, were of gold. And the damsel was arrayed
in a dress of yellow satin. And she went up to
Owain, and took the ring from off his hand. "Thus,"
said she, "shall be treated the deceiver, the traitor,
the faithless, the disgraced, and the beardless." [1] And
she turned her horse's head, and departed.

Then his adventure came to Owain's remembrance,
and he was sorrowful. And having finished eating,
he went to his own abode, and made preparations that
night. And the next day he arose, but did not go
to the Court, but wandered to the distant parts of the
earth, and to uncultivated mountains. And he remained there until all his apparel was worn out, and
his body was wasted away, and his hair was grown long.
And he went about with the wild beasts, and fed with
them, until they became familiar with him. But at
length he grew so weak, that he could no longer bear

[1] To the disgrace of thy beard.

them company. Then he descended from the mountains to the valley, and came to a park, that was the fairest in the world, and belonged to a widowed Countess.

One day the Countess and her maidens went forth to walk by a lake, that was in the middle of the park. And they saw the form of a man. And they were terrified. Nevertheless they went near him, and touched him, and looked at him. And they saw that there was life in him, though he was exhausted by the heat of the sun. And the Countess returned to the Castle, and took a flask full of precious ointment, and gave it to one of her maidens. " Go with this," said she, "and take with thee yonder horse, and clothing, and place them near the man we saw just now. And anoint him with this balsam, near his heart ; and if there is life in him, he will arise, through the efficacy of this balsam. Then watch what he will do."

And the maiden departed from her, and poured the whole of the balsam upon Owain, and left the horse and the garments hard by, and went a little way off, and hid herself, to watch him. In a short time she saw him begin to move his arms ; and he arose up, and looked at his person, and became ashamed of the unseemliness of his appearance. Then he perceived the horse and the garments, that were near him. And he crept forward till he was able to draw the garments to him from off the saddle. And he clothed himself, and with difficulty mounted the horse. Then the damsel discovered herself to him, and saluted him. And he was rejoiced when he saw her, and enquired of her, what land and what territory that was. " Truly," said the maiden, "a widowed Countess owns yonder Castle ; at the death of her husband,

he left her two Earldoms, but at this day she has
but this one dwelling that has not been wrested from
her, by a young Earl, who is her neighbour, because
she refused to become his wife." "That is pity," said
Owain. And he and the maiden proceeded to the
Castle; and he alighted there, and the maiden con-
ducted him to a pleasant chamber, and kindled a fire,
and left him.

And the maiden came to the Countess, and gave
the flask into her hand. "Ha! maiden," said the
Countess, "where is all the balsam?" "Have I not
used it all?" said she. "Oh, maiden," said the
Countess, "I cannot easily forgive thee this; it is
sad for me to have wasted seven-score pounds' worth
of precious ointment, upon a stranger whom I know
not. However, maiden, wait thou upon him, until he
is quite recovered."

And the maiden did so, and furnished him with
meat and drink, and fire, and lodging, and medica-
ments, until he was well again. And in three months
he was restored to his former guise, and became even
more comely, than he had ever been before.

One day Owain heard a great tumult, and a sound
of arms in the Castle, and he enquired of the maiden
the cause thereof. "The Earl," said she, "whom I
mentioned to thee, has come before the Castle, with
a numerous army, to subdue the Countess." And
Owain enquired of her whether the Countess had a
horse and arms, in her possession. "She has the
best in the world," said the maiden. "Wilt thou go
and request the loan of a horse and arms for me,"
said Owain, "that I may go and look at this army?"
"I will," said the maiden.

And she came to the Countess, and told her what
Owain had said. And the Countess laughed.

"Truly," said she, "I will even give him a horse and arms, for ever; such a horse and such arms, had he never yet, and I am glad that they should be taken by him to-day, lest my enemies should have them against my will to-morrow. Yet I know not what he would do with them."

The Countess bade them bring out a beautiful black steed, upon which was a beechen saddle, and a suit of armour, for man and horse. And Owain armed himself, and mounted the horse, and went forth, attended by two pages completely equipped, with horses and arms. And when they came near to the Earl's army, they could see neither its extent, nor its extremity. And Owain asked the pages in which troop the Earl was. "In yonder troop," said they, "in which are four yellow standards. Two of them are before, and two behind him." "Now," said Owain, "do you return and await me near the portal of the Castle." So they returned, and Owain pressed forward, until he met the Earl. And Owain drew him completely out of his saddle, and turned his horse's head towards the Castle, and, though it was with difficulty, he brought the Earl to the portal, where the pages awaited him. And in they came. And Owain presented the Earl as a gift to the Countess. And said to her, "Behold a requittal to thee for thy blessed balsam."

The army encamped around the Castle. And the Earl restored to the Countess the two Earldoms, he had taken from her, as a ransom for his life; and for his freedom, he gave her the half of his own dominions, and all his gold, and his silver, and his jewels, besides hostages.

And Owain took his departure. And the Countess and all her subjects besought him to remain, but

Owain chose rather to wander through distant lands
and deserts.

And as he journed, he heard a loud yelling in a
wood.   And it was repeated a second and a third
time.   And Owain went towards the spot, and behold
a huge craggy mound, in the middle of the wood;

on the side of which was a grey rock.   And there was
a cleft in the rock, and a serpent was within the cleft.
And near the rock, stood a black lion, and every time
the lion sought to go thence, the serpent darted
towards him to attack him.   And Owain unsheathed
his sword, and drew near to the rock; and as the
serpent sprung out, he struck him with his sword,
and cut him in two.   And he dried his sword, and
went on his way, as before.   But behold the lion followed him, and played about him, as though it had
been a greyhound, that he had reared.

They proceeded thus throughout the day, until the evening. And when it was time for Owain to take his rest, he dismounted, and turned his horse loose in a flat and wooded meadow. And he struck fire, and when the fire was kindled, the lion brought him fuel enough to last for three nights. And the lion disappeared. And presently the lion returned, bearing a fine large roebuck. And he threw it down before Owain, who went towards the fire with it.

And Owain took the roebuck, and skinned it, and placed collops of its flesh upon skewers, around the fire. The rest of the buck he gave to the lion to devour. While he was doing this, he heard a deep sigh near him, and a second, and a third. And Owain called out to know whether the sigh he heard proceeded from a mortal; and he received answer, that it did. "Who art thou?" said Owain. "Truly," said the voice, "I am Luned, the hand-maiden of the Countess of the Fountain." "And what dost thou here?" said Owain. "I am imprisoned," said she, "on account of the knight who came from Arthur's Court, and married the Countess. And he staid a shor⸱ time with her, but he afterwards departed for the Court of Arthur, and he has not returned since. And he, was the friend I loved best in the world. And ⸲wo of the pages of the Countess's chamber, traduced him, and called him a deceiver. And I told them that they two were not a match for him alone. So they imprisoned me in the stone vault, and said that I should be put to death, unless he came himself, to deliver me, by a certain day; and that is no further off, than the day after to-morrow. And I have no one to send to seek him for me. And his name is Owain the son of Urien." "And art thou certain, that if that knight knew all this, he would come to thy rescue?" "I am most certain of it," said she.

When the collops were cooked, Owain divided them into two parts, between himself and the maiden; and after they had eaten, they talked together until the day dawned. And the next morning Owain enquired of the damsel, if there was any place where he could get food and entertainment for that night. "There is, lord," said she; "cross over yonder, and go along the side of the river, and in a short time, thou wilt see a great Castle, in which are many towers. And the Earl who owns that Castle, is the most hospitable man in the world. There thou mayest spend the night."

Never did sentinel keep stricter watch over his lord, than the lion that night over Owain.

And Owain accoutred his horse, and passed across by the ford, and came in the sight of the Castle. And he entered it, and was honourably received. And his horse was well cared for, and plenty of fodder was placed before him. Then the lion went and laid down in the horse's manger; so that none of the people of the Castle dared to approach him. The treatment which Owain met with there, was such as he had never known elsewhere, for every one was as sorrowful, as though death had been upon him.[1] And they went to meat. And the Earl sat upon one side of Owain; and on the other side his only daughter. And Owain had never seen any more lovely than she. Then the lion came and placed himself between Owain's feet, and he fed him with every kind of food, that he took himself. And he never saw any thing equal to the sadness of the people.

[1] Owen was certain he had never seen better service, but every one was as sorrowful as if death had been upon him.

In the middle of the repast, the Earl began to bid
Owain welcome. "Then," said Owain, "behold it
is time for thee to be cheerful." "Heaven knows,"
said the Earl, "that it is not thy coming that makes
us sorrowful, but we have cause enough for sadness
and care." "What is that?" said Owain. "I have
two sons," replied the Earl, "and yesterday they went
to the mountains to hunt. Now there is on the
mountain a monster, who kills men and devours
them. And he seized my sons. And to-morrow is
the time he has fixed to be here, and he threatens
that he will then slay my sons before my eyes, unless
I will deliver into his hands this my daughter.[1] He
has the form of a man, but in stature he is no less
than a giant."

"Truly," said Owain, "that is lamentable. And
which wilt thou do?" "Heaven knows," said the Earl,
"it will be better that my sons should be slain, against
my will, than I should voluntarily give up my daughter
to him to ill-treat and destroy." Then they talked
about other things, and Owain staid there that night.

The next morning, they heard an exceeding great
clamour, which was caused by the coming of the
giant, with the two youths. And the Earl was anxious
both to protect his Castle, and to release his two sons.[2]
Then Owain put on his armour, and went forth to
encounter the giant; and the lion followed him. And
when the giant saw that Owain was armed, he rushed
towards him, and attacked him. And the lion fought
with the giant, much more fiercely than Owain did.

---

[1] And to-morrow is the appointed day for me to meet him,
to deliver to him yonder maiden, otherwise he will kill my sons
before my eyes.

[2] And the Earl determined to hold the castle against him,
abandoning his two sons to their fate.

Truly," said the giant, "I should find no difficulty in fighting with thee, were it not for the animal that is with thee." Upon that Owain took the lion back to the Castle, and shut the gate upon him. And then he returned to fight the giant, as before. And the lion roared very loud, for he heard that it went hard with Owain. And he climbed up, till he reached the top of the Earl's Hall; and thence he got to the top of the Castle, and he sprang down from the walls, and went and joined Owain. And the lion gave the giant a stroke with his paw, which tore him from his shoulder to his hip, and his heart was laid bare. And the giant fell down dead. Then Owain restored the two youths to their father.

The Earl besought Owain to remain with him, and he would not, but set forward towards the meadow, where Luned was. And when he came there, he saw a great fire kindled, and two youths with beautiful curling auburn hair, were leading the maiden to cast her into the fire. And Owain asked them what charge they had against her. And they told him of the compact[1] that was between them; as the maiden had done the night before. "And," said they, "Owain has failed her, therefore we are taking her to be burnt." "Truly," said Owain, "he is a good knight, and if he knew that the maiden was in such peril, I marvel that he came not to her rescue. But if you will accept me in his stead, I will do battle with you." "We will," said the youths, "by him who made us."

And they attacked Owain, and he was hard beset by them. And with that the lion came to Owain's assistance; and they two got the better of the young men. And they said to him, "Chieftain, it was not

[1] And they told him their tale.

agreed that we should fight, save with thyself alone, and it is harder for us to contend with yonder animal, than with thee." And Owain put the lion in the place where the maiden had been imprisoned, and blocked up the door with stones. And he went to fight with the young men as before. But Owain had not his usual strength,[1] and the two youths pressed hard upon him. And the lion roared incessantly at seeing Owain in trouble. And he burst through the wall, until he found a way out, and rushed upon the young men, and instantly slew them. So Luned was saved from being burned.

Then Owain returned with Luned, to the dominions of the Countess of the Fountain. And when he went thence, he took the Countess with him to Arthur's Court, and she was his wife as long as she lived.

And they took the road that led to the Court of the savage black man. And Owain fought with him, and the lion did not quit Owain, until he had vanquished him. And when he reached the Court of the savage black man, he entered the hall : and beheld four and twenty ladies, the fairest that could be seen. And the garments which they had on, were not worth four and twenty pence. And they were as sorrowful as death. And Owain asked them the cause of their sadness. And they said, "We are the daughters of Earls, and we all came here, with our husbands, whom we dearly loved. And we were received with honour and rejoicing. And we were thrown into a state of stupor, and while we were thus, the demon who owns this Castle, slew all our husbands, and took from us our horses, and our raiment, and our gold, and our silver. And the corpses of our husbands are still in this house, and many others with them. And this,

---

[1] But Owen's strength had not yet returned.

Chieftain, is the cause of our grief, and we are sorry that thou art come hither, lest harm should befall thee."

And Owain was grieved, when he heard this. And he went forth from the Castle, and he beheld a Knight approaching him, who saluted him, in a friendly and cheerful manner, as if he had been a brother. And this was the savage black man. "In very sooth," said Owain, "it is not to seek thy friendship that I am here." "In sooth," said he, "thou shalt not find it then." And with that they charged each other, and fought furiously. And Owain overcame him, and bound his hands behind his back. Then the black savage besought Owain to spare his life, and spoke thus, "My lord Owain," said he, "it was foretold, that thou shouldst come hither and vanquish me, and thou hast done so. I was a robber here, and my house was a house of spoil. But grant me my life, and I will become the keeper of an Hospice, and I will maintain this house as an Hospice for weak and for strong, as long as I live, for the good of thy soul." And Owain accepted the proposal of him, and remained there that night.

And the next day he took the four and twenty ladies, and their horses, and their raiment, and what they possessed of goods, and jewels, and proceeded with them to Arthur's Court. And if Arthur was rejoiced when he saw him, after he had lost him the first time, his joy was now much greater. And of those ladies, such as wished to remain in Arthur's Court, remained there; and such as wished to depart, departed.

And thenceforward Owain dwelt at Arthur's Court, greatly beloved as the head of his household, until he went away with his followers; and those were the

army of three hundred ravens which Kenverchyn had
left him.   And wherever Owain went with these, he
was victorious.

And this is the tale of THE LADY OF THE
FOUNTAIN.

THE DREAM OF RHONABWY.

MADAWÇ the son of Maredudd possessed Powys
within its boundaries, from Porfoed to Gwauan in
the uplands of Arwystli. And at that time he
had a brother, Iorwerth the son of Maredudd,
in rank not equal to himself. And Iorwerth had
great sorrow and heaviness because of the honour
and power that his brother enjoyed, which he shared

not. And he sought his fellows and his foster-brothers, and took counsel with them what he should do in this matter. And they resolved to despatch some of their number to go and seek a maintenance for him. Then Madawc offered him to become Master of the Household and to have horses, and arms, and honour, and to fare like as himself. But Iorwerth refused this.

And Iorwerth made an inroad into England, slaying the inhabitants, and burning houses, and carrying away prisoners. And Madawc took counsel with the men of Powys, and they determined to place an hundred men in each of the three Commots of Powys to seek for him. And thus did they in the plains of Powys from Aber Ceirawc, and in Allictwn Ver, and in Rhyd Wilure, on the Vyrnwy, the three best Commots of Powys. So he was none the better, he nor his household, in Powys, nor in the plains thereof.[1] And they spread these men over the plains as far as Nillystwn Trevan.

Now one of the men who was upon this quest was called Rhonabwy. And Rhonabwy and Kynwrig Vrychgoch, a man of Mawddwy, and Cadwgan Vras, a man of Moelvre in Kynlleith, came together to the house of Heilyn Goch the son of Cadwgan the son of Iddon. And when they near to the house, they saw an old hall, very black and having an upright gable, whence issued a great smoke ; and on entering, they found the floor full of puddles and mounds ; and it was difficult to stand thereon, so slippery was it

---

[1] And they reckoned that the corn land of Powys, from Aber Ceirawc in Allictun Ver to Rhyd Wilure on the Vyrnwy, was as good as the three best commots in Powys ; and that, if there was not sustenance for him and his followers in that corn land, there would be none in Powys.

with the mire of cattle. And where the puddles were a man might go up to his ankles in water and dirt. And there were boughs of holly spread over the floor whereof the cattle had browsed the sprigs. When they came to the hall of the house, they beheld cells full of dust, and very gloomy,[1] and on one side an old hag making a fire. And whenever she felt cold, she cast a lapful of chaff upon the fire, and raised such a smoke, that it was scarcely to be borne, as it rose up the nostrils. And on the other side was a yellow calf skin on the floor, a main privilege was it to any one who should get upon that hide.

And when they had sat down, they asked the hag where were the people of the house. And the hag spoke not but muttered. Thereupon behold the people of the house entered; a ruddy, clownish curly-headed man, with a burthen of fagots on his back, and a pale slender woman, also carrying a bundle under her arm. And they barely welcomed the men, and kindled a fire with the boughs. And the woman cooked something and gave them to eat, barley bread, and cheese, and milk and water.

And there arose a storm of wind and rain, so that it was hardly possible to go forth with safety. And being weary with their journey, they laid themselves down and sought to sleep. And when they looked at the couch, it seemed to be made but of a little coarse straw full of dust and vermin, with the stems of boughs sticking up therethrough, for the cattle had eaten all the straw that was placed at the head and the foot. And upon it was stretched an old russet-coloured rug, threadbare and ragged; and a coarse sheet, full of slits was upon the rug, and an ill-stuffed pillow, and a worn-out cover upon the sheet. And

[1] Scantly draped, poverty-stricken.

after much suffering from the vermin, and from the discomfort of their couch, a heavy sleep fell on Rhonabwy's companions. But Rhonabwy, not being able either to sleep or to rest, thought he should suffer less if he went to lie upon the yellow calf skin that was stretched out on the floor. And there he slept.

As soon as sleep had come upon his eyes, it seemed to him that he was journeying with his companions across the plain of Argyngroeg, and he thought that he went towards Rhyd y Groes on the Severn. As he journeyed, he heard a mighty noise, the like whereof heard he never before; and looking behind him, he beheld a youth with yellow curling hair, and with his beard newly trimmed, mounted on a chesnut horse, whereof the legs were grey from the top of the forelegs, and from the bend of the hindlegs downwards. And the rider wore a coat of yellow satin sewn with green silk, and on his thigh was a gold-hilted sword, with a scabbard of new leather of Cordova, belted with the skin of the deer, and clasped with gold. And over this was a scarf of yellow satin wrought with green silk, the borders whereof were likewise green. And the green of the caparison of the horse, and of his rider, was as green as the leaves of the fir tree, and the yellow was as yellow as the blossom of the broom. So fierce was the aspect of the knight, that fear seized upon them, and they began to flee. And the knight pursued them. And when the horse breathed forth, the men became distant from him, and when he drew in his breath, they were drawn near to him, even to the horse's chest. And when he had overtaken them, they besought his mercy. "You have it gladly!" said he, "fear nought." "Ha, chieftain, since thou hast

mercy upon me, tell me also who thou art," said
Rhonabwy. "I will not conceal my lineage from
thee. I am Iddawc the son of Mynyo, yet not by my
name, but by my nickname am I best known." "And
wilt thou tell us what thy nickname is?" "I will tell
you; it is Iddawc Cordd Prydain." "Ha, chieftain,"
said Rhonabwy, "why art thou called thus?" "I
will tell thee. I was one of the messengers between
Arthur and Medrawd his nephew, at the battle of
Camlan; and I was then a reckless youth, and
through my desire for battle, I kindled strife between
them, and stirred up wrath, when I was sent by
Arthur the Emperor to reason with Medrawd, and to
shew him, that he was his foster-father and his uncle,
and to seek for peace, lest the sons of the Kings of
the Island of Britain, and of the nobles, should be
slain. And whereas Arthur charged me with the
fairest sayings he could think of, I uttered unto
Medrawd the harshest I could devise. And therefore
am I called Iddawc Cordd Prydain, for from this did
the battle of Camlan ensue. And three nights before
the end of the battle of Camlan I left them, and went
to the Llech Las in North Britain to do penance.
And there I remained doing penance seven years, and
after that I gained pardon."

Then lo! they heard a mighty sound which was
much louder than that which they had heard before,
and when they looked round towards the sound;
behold a ruddy youth, without beard or whiskers,[1]
noble of mien, and mounted on a stately courser.
And from the shoulders and the front of the knees
downwards the horse was bay. And upon the man
was a dress of red satin wrought with yellow silk, and
yellow were the borders of his scarf. And such parts

---

[1] Moustache.

of his apparel and of the trappings of his horse as were yellow, as yellow were they as the blossom of the broom, and such as were red, were as ruddy as the ruddiest blood in the world.

Then behold the horseman overtook them, and he asked of Iddawc a share of the little men that were with him. "That which is fitting for me to grant I will grant, and thou shalt be a companion to them as I have been." And the horseman went away. "Iddawc," enquired Rhonabwy, "who was that horseman?" "Rhuvawn Pebyr, the son of Prince Deorthach."

And they journeyed over the plain of Argyngroeg as far as the ford of Rhyd y Groes on the Severn. And for a mile around the ford on both sides of the road, they saw tents and encampments, and there was the clamour of a mighty host. And they came to the edge of the ford, and there they beheld Arthur sitting on a flat island below the ford, having Bedwini[1] the Bishop on one side of him, and Gwarthegyd the son of Kaw on the other. And a tall auburn-haired youth stood before him, with his sheathed sword in his hand, and clad in a coat and a cap of jet black satin. And his face was white as ivory, and his eyebrows black as jet, and such part of his wrist as could be seen between his glove and his sleeve was whiter than the lily, and thicker than a warrior's ankle.

Then came Iddawc and they that were with him, and stood before Arthur, and saluted him. "Heaven grant thee good," said Arthur. "And where, Iddawc, didst thou find these little men?" "I found them, lord, up yonder on the road." Then the Emperor smiled. "Lord," said Iddawc, "wherefore dost thou laugh?" "Iddawc," replied Arthur, "I laugh not;

[1] Bedwin.

but it pitieth me that men of such stature as these should have this Island in their keeping, after the men that guarded it of yore." Then said Iddawc, " Rhonabwy, dost thou see the ring with a stone set in it, that is upon the Emperor's hand?" " I see it," he answered. "It is one of the properties of that stone, to enable thee to remember that thou seest here to-night, and hadst thou not seen the stone, thou wouldest never have been able to remember aught thereof."

After this they saw a troop coming towards the ford. "Iddawc," enquired Rhonabwy, "to whom does yonder troop belong?" "They are the fellows of Rhuvawn Pebyr the son of Prince Deorthach. And these men are honourably served with mead and bragget, and are freely beloved by the daughters of the kings of the Island of Britain. And this they merit, for they were ever in the front and the rear in every peril." And he saw but one hue upon the men and the horses of this troop, for they were all as red as blood. And when one of the knights rode forth from the troop, he looked like a pillar of fire glancing athwart the sky. And this troop encamped above the ford.

Then they beheld another troop coming towards the ford, and these from their horses' chests upwards were whiter than the lily, and below blacker than jet. And they saw one of these knights go before the rest, and spur his horse into the ford in such a manner that the water dashed over Arthur and the Bishop, and those holding counsel with them, so that they were as wet as if they had been drenched in the river. And as he turned the head of his horse, the youth who stood before Arthur struck the horse over the nostrils with his sheathed sword, so that had it been

H

with the bare blade it would have been a marvel if the
bone had not been wounded as well as the flesh.
And the knight drew his sword half out of the
scabbard, and asked of him, "Wherefore didst thou
strike my horse? Whether was it in insult or in
counsel unto me?"   "Thou dost indeed lack
counsel.   What madness caused thee to ride so
furiously as to dash the water of the ford over Arthur,
and the consecrated Bishop, and their counsellors, so
that they were as wet as if they had been dragged out
of the river?"   "As counsel then will I take it."   So
he turned his horse's head round towards his army.

"Iddawc," said Rhonabwy, "who was yonder
knight?"   "The most eloquent and the wisest youth
that is in this Island; Adaon the son of Taliesin."
"Who was the man that struck his horse?"   "A
youth of froward nature; Elphin the son of
Gwyddno."

Then spake a tall and stately man, of noble and
flowing speech, saying that it was a marvel that so
vast a host should be assembled in so narrow a space,
and that it was a still greater marvel that those should
be there at that time who had promised to be
by mid-day in the battle of Badon, fighting with
Osla Gyllellvawr.   "Whether thou mayest choose to
proceed or not, I will proceed."   "Thou sayest
well," said Arthur, "and we will go all together."
"Iddawc," said Rhonabwy, "who was the man who
spoke so marvellously unto Arthur erewhile?"   "A
man who may speak as boldly as he listeth, Caradawc
Vreichvras, the son of Llyr Marini, his chief counsellor
and his cousin."

Then Iddawc took Rhonabwy behind him on his
horse, and that mighty host moved forward, each
troop in its order, towards Cevndigoll.   And when

they came to the middle of the ford of the Severn,
Iddawc turned his horse's head, and Rhonabwy
looked along the valley of the Severn. And he
beheld two fair troops coming towards the ford. One
troop there came of brilliant white, whereof every one
of the men had a scarf of white satin with jet black
borders. And the knees and the tops of the
shoulders of their horses were jet black, though they
were of a pure white in every other part. And their
banners were pure white, with black points to them
all.

"Iddawc," said Rhonabwy, "who are yonder pure
white troop?" "They are the men of Norway, and
March the son of Meirchion is their prince. And he is
cousin unto Arthur." And further on he saw a troop,
whereof each man wore garments of jet black, with
borders of pure white to every scarf; and the tops of
the shoulders and the knees of their horses were pure
white. And their banners were jet black with pure
white at the point of each.

"Iddawc," said Rhonabwy, "who are the jet black
troop yonder?" "They are the men of Denmark, and
Edeyrn the son of Nudd is their prince."

And when they had overtaken the host, Arthur and
his army of mighty ones dismounted below Caer
Badon, and he perceived that he and Iddawc
journeyed the same road as Arthur. And after they
had dismounted he heard a great tumult and
confusion amongst the host, and such as were then at
the flanks, turned to the centre, and such as had
been in the centre moved to the flanks. And then,
behold, he saw a knight coming, clad, both he and
his horse, in mail, of which the rings were whiter than
the whitest lily, and the rivets redder than the ruddies
blood. And he rode amongst the host.

"Iddawc," said Rhonabwy, "will yonder host flee?"
"King Arthur never fled, and if this discourse of thine
were heard, thou wert a lost man. But as to the
knight whom thou seest yonder, it is Kai. The
fairest horseman is Kai in all Arthur's Court; and the
men who are at the front of the army hasten to the
rear to see Kai ride, and the men who are in the
centre, flee to the side from the shock of his horse.[1]
And this is the cause of the confusion of the host."

Thereupon they heard a call made for Kadwr, Earl
of Cornwall, and behold he arose with the sword of
Arthur in his hand. And the similitude of two
serpents was upon the sword in gold. And when the
sword was drawn from its scabbard, it seemed as if
two flames of fire burst forth from the jaws of the
serpents, and then, so wonderful was the sword, that
it was hard for any one to look upon it. And the
host became still, and the tumult ceased, and the
Earl returned to the tent.

"Iddawc," said Rhonabwy, "who is the man who
bore the sword of Arthur?" "Kadwr, the Earl of
Cornwall, whose duty is to arm the King on the days
of battle and warfare."

And they heard a call made for Eirynwych
Amheibyn, Arthur's servant, a red, rough, ill-favoured
man, having red whiskers[2] with bristly hairs. And
behold he came upon a tall red horse, with the mane
parted on each side, and he brought with him a large
and beautiful sumpter pack. And the huge red youth
dismounted before Arthur, and he drew a golden
chair out of the pack, and a carpet of diapered satin.
And he spread the carpet before Arthur, and there
was an apple of ruddy gold at each corner thereof,

---

[1] For fear of being crushed by his horse.
[2] A red moustache.

and he placed the chair upon the carpet. And so large was the chair that three armed warriors might have sat therein. Gwenn was the name of the carpet, and it was ·one of its properties, that whoever was upon it no one could see him, and he could see every one. And it would retain no colour but its own.

And Arthur sat within the carpet, and Owain the

son of Urien was standing before him. "Owain," said Arthur, "wilt thou play chess?" "I will, Lord," said Owain. And the red youth brought the chess for Arthur and Owain ; golden pieces and a board of silver. And they began to play.

And while they were thus, and when they were best amused with their game, behold they saw a white tent with a red canopy, and the figure of a jet black

serpent on the top of the tent, and red glaring
venomous eyes in the head of the serpent, and a red
flaming tongue. And there came a young page with
yellow curling hair, and blue eyes, and a newly
springing beard, wearing a coat and a surcoat of
yellow satin, and hose of thin greenish yellow cloth
upon his feet, and over his hose shoes of parti-
coloured leather, fastened at the insteps with golden
clasps. And he bore a heavy three-edged sword with
a golden hilt, in a scabbard of black leather tipped
with fine gold. And he came to the place where the
Emperor and Owain were playing at chess.

And the youth saluted Owain. And Owain
marvelled that the youth should salute him and should
not have saluted the Emperor Arthur. And Arthur
knew what was in Owain's thought. And he said to
Owain, "Marvel not that the youth salutes thee now,
for he saluted me erewhile; and it is unto thee that
his errand is." Then said the youth unto Owain,
"Lord, is it with thy leave that the young pages and
attendants of the Emperor harass and torment and
worry the Ravens? And if it be not with thy leave,
cause the Emperor to forbid them." "Lord," said
Owain, "thou hearest what the youth says; if it seem
good to thee, forbid them from my Ravens." "Play
thy game," said he. Then the youth returned to the
tent.

That game did they finish, and another they began,
and when they were in the midst of the game, behold,
a ruddy young man with auburn curling hair, and
large eyes, well grown, and having his beard new shorn,
came forth from a bright yellow tent, upon the summit
of which was the figure of a bright red lion. And he
was clad in a coat of yellow satin, falling as low as the
small of his leg, and embroidered with threads of red

silk. And on his feet were hose of fine white
buckram, and buskins of black leather were over his
hose, whereon were golden clasps. And in his hand
a huge, heavy, three-edged sword, with a scabbard of
red-deer hide, tipped with gold. And he came to the
place where Arthur and Owain were playing at chess.
And he saluted him. And Owain was troubled at his
salutation, but Arthur minded it no more than before.
And the youth said unto Owain, "Is it not against
thy will that the attendants of the Emperor harass thy
Ravens, killing some and worrying others? If against
thy will it be, beseech him to forbid them." "Lord,"
said Owain, "forbid thy men if it seem good to thee."
"Play thy game," said the Emperor. And the youth
returned to the tent.

And that game was ended, and another begun.
And as they were beginning the first move of the
game, they beheld at a small distance from them a
tent speckled yellow, the largest ever seen, and the
figure of an eagle of gold upon it, and a precious
stone on the eagle's head. And coming out of the
tent, they saw a youth with thick yellow hair upon his
head, fair and comely, and a scarf of blue satin upon
him, and a brooch of gold in the scarf upon his right
shoulder as large as a warrior's middle finger. And
upon his feet were hose of fine Totness, and shoes of
parti-coloured leather, clasped with gold, and the
youth was of noble bearing, fair of face, with ruddy
cheeks and large hawk's eyes. In the hand of the
youth was a mighty lance, speckled yellow, with a
newly sharpened head; and upon the lance a banner
displayed.

Fiercely angry, and with rapid pace, came the
youth to the place where Arthur was playing at chess
with Owain. And they perceived that he was wroth.

And thereupon he saluted Owain, and told him that his Ravens had been killed, the chief part of them, and that such of them as were not slain were so wounded and bruised that not one of them could raise its wings a single fathom above the earth. "Lord," said Owain, "forbid thy men." "Play," said he "if it please thee." Then said Owain to the youth, "Go back, and wherever thou findest the strife at the thickest, there lift up the banner, and let come what pleases Heaven." So the youth returned back to the place where the strife bore hardest upon the Ravens, and he lifted up the banner; and as he did so they all rose up in the air, wrathful and fierce and high of spirit, clapping their wings in the wind, and shaking off the weariness that was upon them. And recovering their energy and courage, furiously and with exultation did they, with one sweep, descend upon the heads of the men, who had erewhile caused them anger and pain and damage, and they seized some by the heads and others by the eyes, and some by the ears, and others by the arms, and carried them up into the air; and in the air there was a mighty tumult with the flapping of the wings of the triumphant Ravens, and with their croaking; and there was another mighty tumult with the groaning of the men, that were being torn and wounded, and some of whom were slain.

And Arthur and Owain marvelled at the tumult as they played at chess; and, looking, they perceived a knight upon a dun-coloured horse coming towards them. And marvellous was the hue of the dun horse. Bright red was his right shoulder, and from the top of his legs to the centre of his hoof was bright yellow. Both the knight and his horse were fully equipped with heavy foreign armour. The clothing of the horse from the front opening upwards was of bright red sendal, and from thence opening downwards was of bright yellow sendal. A large gold-hilted one-edged sword had the youth upon his thigh, in a scabbard of light blue, and tipped with Spanish laton. The belt of the sword was of dark green leather with golden slides and a clasp of ivory upon it, and a buckle of jet black upon the clasp. A helmet of gold was on the head of the knight, set with precious stones of great virtue, and at the top of the helmet was the image of a flame-coloured leopard with two ruby-red stones in its head, so that it was astounding for a warrior, however stout his heart, to look at the face of the leopard, much more at the face of the knight. He had in his hand a blue-shafted lance, but from the haft to the point it was stained crimson-red, with the blood of the Ravens and their plumage.

The knight came to the place where Arthur and Owain were seated at chess. And they perceived that he was harassed and vexed and weary as he came towards them. And the youth saluted Arthur, and told him, that the Ravens of Owain were slaying his young men and attendants. And Arthur looked at Owain and said, "Forbid thy Ravens." "Lord," answered Owain, "play thy game." And they played. And the knight returned back towards the strife, and the Ravens were not forbade any more than before.

And when they had played awhile, they heard a mighty tumult, and a wailing of men, and a croaking of Ravens, as they carried the men in their strength into the air, and, tearing them betwixt them, let them fall piecemeal to the earth. And during the tumult they saw a knight coming towards them, on a light grey horse, and the left foreleg of the horse was jet black to the centre of his hoof. And the knight and the horse were fully accoutred with huge heavy blue armour.   And a robe of honour of yellow diapered satin was upon the knight, and the borders of the robe were blue.   And the housings of the horse were jet black, with borders of bright yellow.   And on the thigh of the youth was a sword, long, and three-edged, and heavy.   And the scabbard was of red cut leather, and the belt of new red deerskin, having upon it many golden slides and a buckle of the bone of the sea horse, the tongue of which was jet black.   A golden helmet was upon the head of the knight, wherein were set sapphire stones of great virtue.   And

at the top of the helmet was the figure of a flame-coloured lion, with a fiery-red tongue, issuing above a foot from his mouth, and with venomous eyes, crimson-red, in his head.   And the knight came, bearing in his hand a thick ashen lance, the head whereof, which had been newly steeped in blood, was overlaid with silver.

And the youth saluted the Emperor: "Lord," said he, "carest thou not for the slaying of thy pages, and thy young men, and the sons of the nobles of the Island of Britain, whereby it will be difficult to

defend this Island from henceforward for ever?"
"Owain," said Arthur, "forbid thy Ravens." "Play
this game, Lord," said Owain.

So they finished the game, and began another; and
as they were finishing that game, lo, they heard a great
tumult and a clamour of armed men, and a croaking
of Ravens, and a flapping of wings in the air, as they
flung down the armour entire to the ground, and the
men and the horses piecemeal. Then they saw
coming a knight on a lofty-headed piebald horse.
And the left shoulder of the horse was of bright red,
and its right leg from the chest to the hollow of the
hoof was pure white. And the knight and horse were
equipped with arms of speckled yellow, variegated
with Spanish laton. And there was a robe of honour
upon him, and upon his horse, divided in two parts,
white and black, and the borders of the robe of honour
were of golden purple. And above the robe he wore
a sword three-edged and bright, with a golden hilt.
And the belt of the sword was of yellow goldwork,
having a clasp upon it of the eyelid of a black sea
horse, and a tongue of yellow gold to the clasp.
Upon the head of the knight was a bright helmet of
yellow laton, with sparkling stones of crystal in it, and
at the crest of the helmet was the figure of a griffin,
with a stone of many virtues in its head. And he
had an ashen spear in his hand, with a round shaft,
coloured with azure blue. And the head of the spear
was newly stained with blood, and was overlaid with
fine silver.

Wrathfully came the knight to the place where
Arthur was, and he told him that the Ravens had
slain his household and the sons of the chief men of
this Island, and he besought him to cause Owain to
forbid his Ravens. And Arthur besought Owain

to forbid them.   Then Arthur took the golden chessmen that were upon the board, and crushed them
until they became as dust.   Then Owain ordered
Gwres the son of Rheged to lower his banner.   So it
was lowered, and all was peace.

Then Rhonabwy enquired of Iddawc, who were the
first three men that came to Owain, to tell him his
Ravens were being slain.   Said Iddawc, "They were
men who grieved that Owain should suffer loss, his
fellow-chieftains and companions, Selyv the son of
Kynan Garwyn of Powys, and Gwgawn Gleddyvrudd,
and Gwres the son of Rheged, he who bears the
banner in the day of battle and strife."   "Who," said
Rhonabwy, "were the last three men who came to
Arthur, and told him that the Ravens were slaughter-
ing his men?"   "The best of men," said Iddawc,
"and the bravest, and who would grieve exceedingly
that Arthur should have damage in aught; Blathaon,
the son of Mawrheth,[1] and Rhuvawn Pebyr the son of
Prince Deorthach, and Hyveidd Unllenn."

And with that behold four and twenty knights came
from Osla Gyllellvawr, to crave a truce of Arthur for a
fortnight and a month.   And Arthur arose and went
to take counsel.   And he came to where a tall auburn
curly-headed man was a little way off, and there he
assembled his counsellors.   Bedwini,[2] the Bishop, and
Gwarthegyd the son of Kaw, and March the son of
Meirchawn, and Caradawc Vreichvras, and Gwalchmai
the son of Gwyar, and Edeyrn the son of Nudd, and
Rhuvawn Pebyr the son of Prince Deorthach, and
Rhiogan the son of the King of Ireland, and
Gwenwynwyn the son of Nav, Howel the son of
Emyr Llydaw, Gwilym the son of Rhwyf Freinc, and
Daned the son of Ath,[3] and Goreu Custennin, and

[1] Murheth.   [2] Bedwin.   [3] Oth.

Mabon the son of Modron, and Peredur Paladyr Hir, and Hyveidd[1] Unllenn, and Twrch the son of Perif, and Nerth the son of Kadarn, and Gobrwy the son of Echel Vorddwyttwll, Gwair the son of Gwestyl, and Gadwy[2] the son of Geraint, Trystan[3] the son of Tallwch, Moryen Manawc, Granwen the son of Llyr, and Llacheu the son of Arthur, and Llawvrodedd Varvawc, and Kadwr Earl of Cornwall, Morvran the son of Tegid, and Rhyawd the son of Morgant, and Dyvyr the son of Alun Dyved, Gwrhyr Gwalstawd Ieithoedd, Adaon the son of Taliesin, Llary[4] the son of Kasnar[5] Wledig, and Fflewddur Fflam, and Greidawl Galldovydd, Gilbert the son of Kadgyffro, Menw the son of Teirgwaedd, Gwrthmwl Wledig, Cawrdav the son of Caradawc Vreichvras, Gildas the son of Kaw, Kadyriaith the son of Saidi, and many of the men of Norway, and Denmark, and many of the men of Greece, and a crowd of the men of the host came to that counsel.

"Iddawc," said Rhonabwy, "who was the auburn haired man to whom they came just now?" "Rhun the son of Maelgwn Gwynedd, a man of whose prerogative it is, that he may join in counsel with all."[6] "And wherefore did they admit into counsel with men of such dignity as are yonder a stripling so young as Kadyriaith the son of Saidi?" "Because there is not throughout Britain a man better skilled in counsel than he."

Thereupon, behold, bards came and recited verses before Arthur, and no man understood those verses,

[1] Heneidd.   [2] Adwy.   [3] Dyrstan.
[4] Llara.   [5] Kasnat.
[6] It is his privilege that everyone should come to have counsel with him.

but Kadyriaith only, save that they were in Arthur's praise.

And, lo, there came four and twenty asses with their burdens of gold and of silver, and a tired wayworn man with each of them, bringing tribute to Arthur from the Islands of Greece. Then Kadyriaith the son of Saidi besought that a truce might be granted to Osla Gyllellvawr for the space of a fortnight and a month, and that the asses and the burdens they carried might be given to the bards, to be to them as

the reward for their stay and that their verse might be recompensed, during the time of the truce. And thus it was settled.

"Rhonabwy," said Iddawc, "would it not be wrong to forbid a youth who can give counsel so liberal as this from coming to the councils of his Lord?"

Then Kai arose, and he said, "Whosoever will follow Arthur, let him be with him to-night in Cornwall, and whosoever will not, let him be opposed to Arthur even during the truce." And through the

greatness of the tumult that ensued, Rhonabwy awoke.
And when he awoke he was upon the yellow calf skin,
having slept three nights and three days.

And this tale is called The Dream of Rhonabwy.
And this is the reason that no one knows the dream
without a book, neither bard nor gifted seer; because
of the various colours that were upon the horses, and
the many wondrous colours of the arms and of the
panoply, and of the precious scarfs, and of the virtue-
bearing stones.